KU-388-837

Apple Tree Cottage

Also by Rose Boucheron

By the River
Birch Common
Inverness Square
A Secret in the Family
Farewells
The Butterfly Field
Victoria's Emeralds
Secrets of the Past
The Patchwork Quilt
Promise of Summer
Friend and Neighbours
The Massinghams
September Fair
The End of a Long Summer
Pollen

Apple Tree Cottage

Rose Boucheron

All the characters in this book are fictitious and any resemblance to real persons, living or dead, is entirely coincidental.

First published in Great Britain in 2005 by
Judy Piatkus (Publishers) Ltd of
5 Windmill Street, London W1T 2JA
email: info@piatkus.co.uk

The moral right of the author has been asserted

A catalogue record for this book is available from the British Library

ISBN 0 7499 0718 5

Set in Times by
Action Publishing Technology Ltd, Gloucester

Printed and bound in Great Britain by
CPI Bath

For Caroline

Chapter One

It was the month of May in the Cotswolds, and the countryside had never looked more beautiful.

Fields stretched far into the distance, fruit orchards were in bud everywhere and as far as the eye could see there were trees. Nowhere in the world, Ruth decided, were the trees as beautiful as in England in May. Chestnuts, now in full bloom, their white and pink cones reaching up to the sky, poplars, ash and oak and lime, all those variable greens, while from cottage gardens laburnum and lilac, almost over, scented the air, and wistaria in all its glory clung to cottage walls.

There seemed to be no reason why the little village on the edge of the Cotswolds should have been called Little Astons – at least not as far as anyone knew. The village itself was almost five hundred years old and had started out with a row of cottages to house farm labourers and men employed in the wool trade in the bigger villages. It had grown over the years, but not a great deal. A manor house, Astons Manor, stood on a beautiful escarpment and could be seen for miles around. It was open to visitors during the summer and was very well patronised. A Georgian house, now a nursing home, stood at the end of Notcutts Lane; there was a row of little cottages on the main street, and narrow turnings which straggled off. Not many tourists came to Little Astons, there being more to see in the nearby famous and prestigious villages that people flocked to from all over the world. But if they had bothered to find it, they would have seen it was quite enchanting in a small way, an interesting little place, historic, with a small church, hardly big enough to be called one, a chapel, and a village hall, alongside a few houses at each end of the village.

Ruth Durling had recently bought an empty cottage in Notcutts Lane after the death of her husband John eight months previously, and was trying hard to get used to it; to the move into a smaller house, the loss of John and the complete changeover from one environment to another.

They had lived in a house just outside Cheltenham all their married lives, John being at the Foreign Office, but they had always promised themselves that when he retired they would move into the Cotswolds. However, it was not to be, for John's untimely death at the age of sixty-four had shattered their plans. He had seemed the sort of man to go on for ever, never having been ill in his life, and they had been looking forward to many more years together. Ruth was still not used to the fact that he had suddenly been taken from her. In one day she had gone from being a happy wife to a grieving widow, and yet people said she was lucky. How much worse if she had had to spend months, years even, caring for a loved one. But the shock took some getting used to. Both her sons worked abroad and her daughter Alice lived a few miles away in Cheltenham.

Well, she would have to get used to it, having taken the plunge. The cottage seemed so small, cramped even after a house, but what was the use of staying on there after John had gone?

Now she seemed to be fairly straight, and thanked God for Alice. She was so efficient. Everything was where it should be, whereas Ruth would have taken hours to unpack, examining everything and staring at it while the tears poured down her face.

'Plenty of room,' Alice said. 'Daddy would have approved.'

Actually, he wouldn't, but she was only trying to help. If there was anything John hated it was being cramped. John loved lots of space, and the small garden would not have appealed at all. They had had a large garden, which was John's pride and joy.

Ruth opened the kitchen cupboards – almost bare, all her little pots and jars reposing in the waste bin.

'Ma!' Alice said. 'October 1999—'

'Well, I don't use it much now—'

'How long have you had these cinnamon sticks?' Alice asked accusingly.

'Auntie Louise brought them back from – oh, I forget where – the West Indies – years ago—'

'You can say that again,' she said grimly. 'Ten at least.'

'But I'm fond of them, even though I don't use them—'

'Buy some more,' Alice said. 'Fresh. Cocoa – I never saw you use cocoa – sell-by date, now let's see.' She was enjoying this.

'Year 2000,' she said, binning it. 'Oh, and some soups – you're going to need some fresh ones.' She looked closely at the dates. 'Yes, I thought so,' she said throwing them into the bin which by now was full. 'Semolina?' she said curiously. 'Do you use it?'

Ruth shook her head. 'No—'

'So, stock up on some fresh food, fresh tins, you'll enjoy that – nice new kitchen – they did a good job, I must say.' She looked round approvingly, eyeing the fridge. 'Now, by the way this marmalade is out of date even though it is in the fridge . . .' Ruth began to feel distinctly unhealthy and not a little guilty.

In the bedroom Alice had made the bed with newly laundered sheets and pillows, tidied the dressing table, and put a cushion or two on the bed. Ruth looked out of the window, and it was a lovely view. Outside on the small drive, her car sat in front of Alice's. The long path down to the gate had been widened to take the width of a car.

'Pity you've no garage, still, I'm sure there are plenty of

people who will let a garage if you really wanted one. They'd be glad of the rent . . . now, I'll put the kettle on and we'll have some tea. I made you a fruit cake and brought you some of those little tarts I used to make, do you remember?'

Alice was a cook. A Food Technology teacher and a very good one. Ruth remembered the way she used to get in the kitchen and take over when she was small.

Sometimes she had gone next door to the newly built house with the beautiful modern kitchen to see Mrs Wood who had a wonderful new house with a super kitchen. There was nothing she liked more than trying all those appliances.

She wandered into the living room and saw where Alice had stood the photograph of the two boys and herself, her arms round each shoulder, her one dimple showing. She adored them.

'Now, you'll be all right, won't you?' Alice asked, going out of the front door and getting into her car. 'Just ring me, if you need anything – I'll be over at the weekend.' She started the engine. 'Are you still going up to town on Monday?'

'Yes, I wouldn't miss that,' Ruth said with a false smile, for she *would* miss Alice when she had gone.

After she had closed the door and locked it, she went into the sitting room and sat down quietly, weeping for no reason other than pent-up emotion. Oh, John, she thought, John . . .

After the boys were born she had a miscarriage at ten weeks and was rushed off to hospital for a D and C.

'What's that?' she asked her doctor. She was scared stiff. She had never been a brave woman where health was concerned.

'Think of it as a cosmetic operation,' he said kindly. He was Irish and such a nice man. A real family doctor. 'You want to be fresh as a daisy for your next baby, don't you?'

John held her tightly to comfort her.

The medical profession had made many discoveries since those days. They took her to a large London hospital which was quite disgusting. It was before the days when they began to thoroughly overhaul hospitals. She was put down on a bed in the centre of the ward because there was no room, surrounded by mothers who had had their babies.

'Are you the abortion?' a nurse said, passing her.

'I am not!' Ruth said, shocked beyond reason. 'I have had a miscarriage.'

'Under three months it's an abortion, love,' the nurse said. 'Now, take her,' and handed Ruth a tiny baby in a shawl from the woman opposite who had just had a seizure of some sort.

Oh, how cruel, she thought, but thank God I have two lovely young sons at home.

It was all over in a matter of minutes and they sent her home.

Pregnant again, at seven months she had a placenta previa. Once more she was whisked off – to another hospital.

'Ah,' the doctor welcomed her, 'the rhesus negative mother.'

Ruth was horrified. 'I am not!' she said. 'I have two perfectly lovely sons at home!'

He gave her a quizzical look. 'Don't look so ashamed!' he said. 'It's just a different kind of blood.'

'Why was I not told when I had my sons?' she asked.

'Well, for whatever reason, that's what you are.'

Her own mother was even more ignorant and had turned her head away. But Ruth was semi-proud of the rhesus-negative bit.

'That's John's family,' her mother said. 'Nothing to do with us.'

'Well, we'll have to see if he is yellow or blue,' the nurse said in this nice new hospital. And there she was, a dear little girl, 'She's fine,' the nurse assured her.

How much we have learned since then, Ruth thought.

When John came in to visit she could see he was really chuffed to have a daughter. 'What shall we call her?'

'Alexandra,' she said. She had always fancied that as a name for a daughter.

But as the days wore on, Ruth just couldn't see her darling daughter as Alexandra. It was far too formal and stiff for her. She was a loving little bundle with one dimple and a round pretty face and smiling eyes. She needed a much more friendly name, and when a congratulations card came saying 'Can't wait to see little Sandy', that was that.

'Alice,' Ruth said, and Alice she became.

She flopped down on to the sofa in the small living room. Now what was she going over all this for? At this late stage. Was she regretting the move already? For of course everything was different. The furniture looked unfamiliar placed in a strange house, John's chair beside an old fireplace. What had she been thinking of? Yet she had been determined to move.

'You shouldn't make a move for at least two years after losing a loved one,' she was told. 'You need that time to make up your mind, to think about it . . .'

But she had been adamant. 'I must get out of here,' she told Alice. 'I can't stay here . . .'

Alice was practical. 'Well, you certainly don't need a large house like this on your own, it's not as if we all come to stay, but don't rush into things. You've plenty of time – take it slowly and think about it.'

But had she? No.

She did what she and John had planned to do. Moved to Little Astons. They had always liked it, both she and John. Perhaps not exactly where the cottage was, but she wanted something small, comfortable. For just one. Apple Tree Cottage. She had thought it just right.

At Montpellier, their house in Cheltenham, so called after their honeymoon in France, she could see John everywhere. She expected him to be in his chair in the living room, upstairs in the bathroom, cutting the lawn. She saw him at every corner of the High Street when she did her shopping. She had had to get away. This was to be her life now, she was on her own.

Sixty-two, she surely still had some life left in her? It was no age today and it would do no good to stay on at Montpellier wishing that John was still there. She must be sensible, make a new life for herself. The boys, flying back to wherever they were, told her to look out for herself – they would phone her, often, be on a plane at the drop of a hat. Alice, left holding the fort, told her not to rush things, but said moving to Little Astons was a good idea. She had to make the move sometime – so why not now. And who knew she would make new friends, take up new interests – so much to do with her life – she was still young . . .

Ruth got up, walked into the hall to look in the mirror. Her face looked strained. Blue shadows under her eyes. Her hair lank, she looked – ravaged. Well, who wouldn't, having lost a husband and a lovely home. Didn't they say moving house and losing a loved one were two of the most stressful things? So it was no wonder she looked like this. She was thin, she had lost some weight, in fact, she looked a mess.

Still, no one was to blame but herself. She had made the decision. It was up to her to make it work.

The trouble was since John had taken early retirement at sixty, they had gone everything together, had had two years of doing everything together. Her women friends had taken a back seat; lots of people were in the same boat. Husbands taking early retirement was not unusual these days, some had gone abroad to live, France, Spain . . .

She hoped to make new friends in Little Astons. She must find something to do. Get busy. She would take care of the garden, keep the house clean herself, no longer have domestic help. That would keep her busy. She looked out through the hall window to see quite a few lights on in the cottages. She had seen one woman, a younger woman, who had come out of one of the cottages when she came to visit with the agent, who had smiled at her and looked pleasant enough. Really, what was she complaining about? The house was a joy. As pretty as a picture, with a lovely garden; it had been newly decorated to her own taste, the furniture had gone in quite well – why then was she so miserable, so stressed?

I'm alone, she thought. But at least I don't expect John to be here with me as I did at Montpellier. I know I'm on my own. I must face up to it. After all, millions of people live alone from choice.

Checking that everything was switched off, slowly she made her way upstairs to the bathroom.

Ruthie, which was what her mother would have called her, thank goodness you are going up to town on Monday. It is a bit quick after the move, but what's to do here? Alice has seen to everything. Julie is just the old friend you want to see after all this. She is good for you, she will make you look better – and feel better. Nothing like an old friend.

To get up to Julie's London flat, the familiar surroundings, to relax and shop around afterwards had once been one of the pleasures of her life. Perhaps, also, Julie would be able to come down and stay now and again. She would look forward to that.

How strange the bedroom looked with its newly built-in wardrobe, her old Victorian dressing table in the window. She had kept the double bed, couldn't bear the idea of sleeping in a single one.

She looked out of the bedroom window, at the fields rising into the distance, she could even see Astons Manor from here, and the apple orchard in front of the house ... There were lights in Notcutts Lane, in Greystones Nursing Home and at the house where the woman lived who had smiled at her; there were no lights next door, but she wasn't alone ...

She pulled the curtains and, picking up her book, snuggled down in her own bed in a strange room. But she couldn't read. It was like being in an hotel room. Presently she put down her book and switched off the light, feeling more strange than she had ever felt. As if she were someone else. Suddenly she burst into tears, weeping convulsively in a way she had never done, not even on the day John had died. Finally, exhausted she fell asleep.

She woke to the sound of birdsong, then a bell ringing at the front door and, going down in her dressing gown, found it was the milkman. A cheery sort, 'obliging' they would have said in the old days and, confronted by an early May morning, at the sunshine on the trees and flowers in the garden, she smiled at him.

Somehow, everything seemed different today. She forgot her feelings of hopelessness of the night before. What had Scarlett O'Hara said? Tomorrow is another day . . .

Chapter Two

With a last look in the mirror, Janet Foster closed the front door of the little cottage in Notcutts Lane and walked down the path bound for the hairdressing session at Greystones Nursing Home.

She half glanced back towards the house where the new woman had moved in yesterday knowing she should have gone and had a word with her, made her welcome, because she seemed to be on her own. But she was late already. She would do it on her way home.

It would be nice to have a new neighbour, although she wasn't all that young from what Janet had seen of her. But an improvement on that poor old man who had been at least ninety and had lived in the house for ever. And goodness knows what she must have spent on the house - new kitchen and outside painted, garden cleared; still it did look nice.

Saturday was her morning for Greystones where she had a hairdressing session. She liked to be busy, and anyway, she had the afternoon off. Young David would be playing football, while Ralph was at college. She enjoyed her weekends, though. Time to catch up with everything.

That woman was probably a widow, though she could have been divorced, you never knew these days. She had never imagined herself ending up as a divorced woman, not in her wildest dreams. She had thought, naïve as she was, that you married for life. But now she had no qualms in admitting to it. Four years – she had almost forgotten what Jack looked like.

Six years ago when the boys were younger they had moved to Spain. Jack was a hairdresser too, and that had been so exciting. Sold up the establishment they had in Stroud, bought a going concern – English need it be said, the owner was retiring, and going back to England because of ill health.

Oh, the hopes they had had! Lovely weather, good business, a wonderful lifestyle – well, that was true to a certain extent. The boys had not been too keen but they would have got used to it. She and Jack got tanned as they never would have in Stroud, Glos., for they lay on the beach in their off moments, and life was wonderful. But it was she who had doubts first. It all seemed too much of a good thing, even though they worked hard, very hard, into the evenings. An afternoon siesta, but busy evenings. And the more the English came to Rospana, the more popular their business became. The fact they were so near to Marbella was a good thing, business wise, for women trekked out to the salon. Jack was obviously having a whale of a time. He was good looking, charming and, she had to say it, a damned fine hairdresser. She had grown up with Jack, so she was inclined to take his good looks and personality for granted, but of course all the women asked for him. Well, that was natural wasn't it. But because she was so busy and involved in the business she did not at first notice that there was more to Jack's charm and his warmth with the customers.

She had to keep an eye on the assistants and train them yet, afterwards, she couldn't believe that she had closed her eyes as to what was going on. When he gave that smile of his in a certain way to a rich woman she had not thought anything of it. Honestly. It was business. But once she became suspicious over what now she couldn't remember, she was alerted and began to watch for signs. And there they were all right.

How could she have been so blind? The trip to Marbella for the Hair Demonstration weekend; well, she couldn't go and leave the boys, not that she wanted to. And that long trip to Seville to see the new man from Italy who had achieved a certain new way of cutting. The extremely wealthy woman who wouldn't leave her villa but insisted on Señor Jack doing her hair. She and Jack were delighted until the rot set in, and she realised that Jack didn't belong to her at all. He belonged to several other women. Her one thought had been her sons.

Well, it was all water under the bridge now. She had taken him for granted, that was the trouble. Stay and continue a life like that? The decision wasn't hard. The boys were only too willing to go home, they missed their friends, and Jack didn't put up much of an argument either, to her chagrin. Well, he wouldn't, would he? He knew when he was well off.

Truth to tell, the life in Spain was not for her. Asked in all honesty, even if Jack had been straight, she would have said, I'd like to go home.

She was English. English to the core. And proud of it. And slow on the uptake, she grinned to herself.

What was she thinking about all this for? She had almost reached Greystones . . .

She was lucky with her own hair. Naturally curly, she had never found it any trouble, short or long. Not for her the strings of bleached hair that hung over the face, or the cropped spikes that made most women look comical, she considered. No, she'd keep her curly locks, whatever the fashion.

'Hair is a woman's crowning glory,' her mother used to say. 'Your hair is a frame for the face.'

And so it was. It was her one claim to natural beauty, the chestnut locks, thick and abundant. As for the rest of her, she wasn't going to complain. She had lost a lot of weight when she and Jack separated, but she was more normal now, having put on a few pounds.

Everyone knew Janet, all the villagers in the small out-of-the-way Cotswold village. Girls she had gone to school with, even the wealthy newcomers, for she worked for them from time to time. She was a good sort, they decided. Reliable, a hard worker, and one with a sense of humour, which always saved the day.

She had reached the nursing home where it stood at the end of Notcutts Lane at the turn into the village. Funny, she thought, I'm suddenly here. For it didn't matter where you were, walking down a lane, sitting in a train, in the bath, you never stopped thinking . . .

It was an impressive house which had seen better days until the end of the Second World War, when it was taken over by a couple who ran it as a nursing home. Since then it had had several owners, but now was run efficiently by a Mrs Woolsbridge, no first names here, who had been a nurse, and who took in ladies of somewhat advanced years, or people whose families did not want them. They had to be over sixty-five, and in reasonably good health, although if they were not chronically ill she would look after them, but her fees were quite considerable. She was always full. As one person died, her place was filled by another, and so it went on.

Janet did half a day a week here on a Saturday as a hairdresser and the residents were always pleased to see her, for she livened the place up.

Now she opened one half of the tall iron gates, hearing it clang behind her, and walked up the drive, her high heels clicking on the new paving. She liked wearing high heels, they made her feel important, although she would change when she got inside the house.

Janet always wore black: trousers and jacket or long coat. Having discovered in the last few years since the death of her mother that it suited her, she wore it always.

She had dark brown eyes and a rosy complexion. You would never have taken her for a townie, and she would have been horrified if you had.

The doorway of Greystones was impressive. Flanked on either side by two lions at the top of a flight of six steps, the huge door was of carved oak, with an impressive brass bell-pull.

There was another small bell at the side which she pressed, and one of the young helpers came to the door, breaking into a grin when she saw who it was.

'Oh, lovely to see you, Janet. They're all waiting.'

'Hello, Rosie.'

Mrs Woolsbridge, who never smiled if she could help it, emerged from the dining room. 'Good morning, Janet,' she said, glancing at her watch. 'Three today, Mrs Bligh, Mrs Bancroft and Miss Willis.' She didn't add, and all dying to see you so they can have a bit of a laugh. She knew Janet cheered them up.

Janet took off her jacket and changed her shoes for flat ones, shrinking in stature as she did so. She took down a white coat from the peg marked 'Mrs Foster' and put it on, greeting several helpers as she did so. Then she made for the two bedrooms on the ground floor. Alongside Mrs Woolsbridge's apartment, the dining room, and the 'lounge', as Mrs Woolsbridge called it, these two were the most expensive.

She tapped on the door of Mrs Bancroft's room and a quiet voice said, 'Come in'.

Mrs Bancroft was sitting just in front of the open window beside her dressing table. 'Ah, Janet dear. I am so glad you came.'

She was a quietly spoken woman with soft grey hair. She was seventy-four years old, and had lived at the home for the last four years, her children not wanting her or, as they said, not having room for her.

She never complained, but accepted her lot, and Janet knew she would not have gone to live with them even if they wanted her. She was very independent, but did not relish living alone. This place was the answer to that problem, Janet thought. If you could afford it, that is.

'Well, what are we going to do today? Shampoo? Trim?'

She put a towel around the woman's shoulders followed by a plastic cape, holding her arm as they walked into the adjoining bathroom.

'No, just a shampoo. This perm seems to be holding well. Do you know, I think I am going to grow my hair long again.'

Janet had heard all this before. Many elderly women felt they wanted all their hair back, but it didn't last long. They would soon ask for a trim – to tidy up the ends ...

With the woman's face staring up at her from the basin, Janet shampooed, rubbing well, for they liked to feel their hair had been really washed, then applied the conditioner, about which they were very fussy.

'How's David?' Mrs Bancroft asked.

'Football today, as usual,' Janet said, wrapping Mrs Bancroft's head in a soft towel.

Then she led her back to the chair in front of the dressing-table mirror. 'We've got a new woman living in our cottages,' she said, knowing the women liked a bit of news.

Mrs Bancroft's eyes were wide, the palest blue, a washed-out blue.

'I haven't spoken to her yet, but she looks nice.'

'Oh, what age would she be?'

'Well,' she hesitated. 'Not young – well – sixty?' she queried, as if Mrs Bancroft would know.

She began to comb through the wet hair. 'She's had a lot done to the house, a new kitchen, painting, garden done.'

'Is she single – a widow?'

'I don't know,' Janet said. 'But I shall call in sometime today. How is your family?' She didn't really care – thought them a shiftless lot. They would be glad enough of the old lady's money when she died.

'Oh,' Mrs Bancroft's face lightened. 'I've heard from

my grandsons – all at college, you know.'

'That's very good.'

'Your son is at university, isn't he? Clever boy.'

'Yes, Birmingham,' Janet said. She dabbed at the drying hair. 'Now, what do you think? Shall we go mad and have lots of curls, Joan Collins, or smooth and chic like –' she sought for a name – 'Shelley in Coronation Street –' knowing they all watched it.

Mrs Bancroft laughed out loud. 'Oh, I don't think so,' she said and they laughed together.

'Happy with the drier?'

'Yes, dear. Not too hot.'

'You know,' Janet said gently moving the drier over her head along with the brush, 'You ought to wear a little make-up – honestly.'

Mrs Bancroft's eyes were wide. 'Make-up? Goodness, I stopped wearing that a long time ago.'

'You'd be surprised what a little touch of lipstick would do for you.'

Mrs Bancroft stared hard at herself in the mirror.

'Let me put on a little bit before I go – just a pale one – nothing vivid – not scarlet.' And they looked at each other in conspiracy.

When she had finished Janet fished a small tube of hand cream out of her bag. 'Now listen, you've got nice hands – and this was a sample – you use it. It feels lovely.'

When she finally left, she saw Mrs Bancroft appraising herself in the mirror. Pouting her lips, and looking down at her hands.

Poor old thing, she thought. 'See you next week . . .'

Next door to Mrs Bligh. A different kettle of fish altogether.

'Allo, love,' Mrs Bligh said.

Mrs Bligh was well built, you might say to be kind, and the widow of the licensee of a big public house in Cirencester. Her diamond rings flashed across the room and her hair was a very distinctive red. She may have been a redhead in her youth, Janet thought it possible, at least she had been fair, but she had been quite white for many a long day. She insisted on this particular red, although Janet often advised her to tone it down.

'You don't like it?' Mrs Bligh looked worried.

'Well, it's a bit – bright,' she said. 'You could go more for auburn.'

Mrs Bligh had made a face. 'Oh, very drab,' she said, and that was that.

'Now,' she smiled broadly at Janet, showing two perfect rows of expensively capped teeth.

'Oh, I've been looking forward to you coming, dear,' she said. 'Just a shampoo today, isn't it? You did my colour last week.'

'Yes, that's right,' Janet said washing her hands.

Today, despite having her hair shampooed, Mrs Bligh was well and truly made up. Janet supposed she was used to it, always having to put a bold front on as a licensee's wife. Her blouse was satin and her skirt much too tight, and she had innumerable strings of pearls and beads round her neck.

She was handsome, though, in a kind of way, and Janet often thought how hard it must be for her, being surprised that she didn't opt for an hotel somewhere where she might have felt more at home. But she was wealthy and a widow, with no children and suffered from 'a touch of the Arthur's' as she called arthritis, and felt happier having some medical care.

Her hands and nails were beautiful. Long, filbert-shaped nails, scarlet painted, slim fingers. A character, Janet thought, that's what made her job so interesting.

Janet chatted about the new neighbour, for Mrs Bligh wanted to know all about her, and whether Janet was going up to see Miss Willis who was having a sulky turn, the carer had said.

'Oh, dear,' Janet sighed. 'Well, we'll have to see if we can pull her out of it.'

'You'll be lucky,' Mrs Bligh said.

Upstairs, Miss Willis greeted her grimly. She kept her back turned to Janet. 'Just a shampoo,' she said.

'Good afternoon, Miss Willis,' Janet said, smiling.

Miss Willis was silent.

'A shampoo . . . It's a lovely day outside . . . Have you been out in the garden?'

'No, much too windy.'

Janet was surprised. She hadn't even noticed a breeze.

'Ah, well,' Miss Willis walked into the bathroom, a tall angular figure, her hair cropped so short as to be almost like a man's. It grew nicely though, a good shape, and Janet enjoyed cutting it, although she did wear it much too short and close to her head.

'Well,' Janet said. 'Have you – been doing anything?' She was going to say exciting, but changed her mind. 'Did you enjoy the book you were reading?'

They kept an excellent library at Greystones and Miss Willis was their most frequent borrower.

There was hardly anything of her hair to shampoo and drying took no time, but Janet kept up a steady flow of nonsense. I wish I could do something for her, she thought. She must be so lonely – hardly speaks to anyone, and I have tried.

'Is there anything you would like from the shops when I go?'

'No, thank you,' Miss Willis said.

Her hair was dry in no time, and Janet thought, she must have been quite good looking when she was younger. Janet knew she was a retired teacher but it was difficult to bring her out of herself.

'Well, you let me know if you need anything,' she said on her way out. 'Anything at all,' she said half heartedly.

'Thank you,' Miss Willis said stiffly.

She walked home thinking about her. How sad she must be. Tightly coiled like a wire. She needed to relax but perhaps that was impossible for her. Perhaps she had always been like that.

She was about to open her gate, when she remembered the new neighbour, and walked along to Apple Tree Cottage.

She noticed how much better the garden looked, weeded, and cut back, the newly painted front door. She knocked and it was answered quickly.

'Oh, hello—' Ruth looked back at her. This was the young woman she had seen before.

Janet held out her hand. 'I'm Janet, Janet Foster,' she said. 'I live just along the road at Plum Tree Cottage.'

Ruth smiled. She was so pleased to see her. 'I'm Ruth Durling,' she said, 'won't you come in?' She held the door wide.

'Oh . . . I'm afraid I can't stop, I have to get back, to get my son's lunch,' Janet smiled. 'But I wanted to say hello and introduce myself since we're neighbours. And if you need anything, you know where I am. Come and have a cup of tea sometime?'

What a kind welcome, Ruth thought. 'How very nice of you. I'd like that.'

'I'll give you a few days to settle in, and I'll give you a call.'

'Thank you.' Ruth watched her walk up the path before closing the door. 'Thank you for dropping by,' she called after her, and Janet turned to wave.

A lady, she thought, by that meaning well spoken and polite, not like some she could mention, and wondered why she had come to Little Astons to live. Lost her husband – or partner – no, he would have been her husband, she was sure. Nice looking, a gentle sort of person, nice grey eyes, pretty smile – probably had children, grown up they would be, and she wasn't that old, sixties, that was nothing these days. After all, she was thirty-nine herself – forty next year, though she didn't want to think about it. Turning the corner, she found her son David, and her eyes lit up.

Oh, you can't beat England, she thought, seeing the little plum tree that she had planted when she moved in in full bloom.

It was warm and sunny, a real late spring day – not like that insufferable heat in Spain. 'Hi, David!' she called. 'Wait for me!'

Chapter Three

Ruth sat in the train on her way to London. It was Monday morning and the train was crowded with day-trippers and commuters. Her appointment with Julie was for eleven am. She was to have an hour-long facial, and afterwards, if things were like they used to be, she would stay for a spot of lunch. In the afternoon she would shop.

As the train sped through the lovely countryside, the rivers now and again in view, flat sparkling areas of water, the overhanging trees, willows and aspen – all went to make a lovely early summer scene.

She had done this journey often from Cheltenham in the past, and there was not a lot of difference in the timing, except that there was no station in Little Astons and she had to make her way to the nearest one by car, leaving it there for the return journey.

This was one of her favourite outings, always had been. Perhaps it was a bit soon after the move, but she had looked forward to seeing London again and her friend Julie. The appointment was made some six weeks ago, for Julie was a busy person. Her mind harked back to the time when she had first met her.

When Alice was a small girl, they would spend one day a month in London, usually in the school holidays, where they would browse through Selfridges until it was time to have Alice's hair cut in the hairdressing salon.

Alice had pretty hair, it grew nicely in a drake's tail at the back, and was thick and chestnut coloured with a hint of red, like Ruth's father's. Ruth wanted to keep the shape, and felt it worth while paying more to have a good hair-dresser to keep it in trim.

While they waited their turn the manageress of the beauty salon often walked through, a tall, handsome woman, her hair pulled back into a chignon, her white coat spotless, lovely dark eyes and high cheekbones.

Ruth glanced out of the window and saw that the view had become more suburban, as the countryside disappeared to give way to housing developments and factories.

She relived those early days. Julie, Miss Pinkerton as she was then – only the junior girl assistants were known by their first names – would stop and say hello and have a chat. Often Ruth felt she would like to indulge in a facial, but she had never been one for beauty treatments.

Over the years, the friendship grew; sometimes she and Julie would have coffee together, until Alice was of an age when she no longer wanted to have her hair cut in town; and she had moved to a new school, where she and all the other pupils wore the latest trends in teenage fashion.

Ruth lost touch then with the trip to the hairdressing salon, although she often felt a desire to go in and ask after Julie Pinkerton. One day some ten years ago, on impulse, she decided to book a facial and learned that Miss Pinkerton had retired, taken early retirement in fact, and the store was being refurbished. They had great plans for the beauty salon.

It was not until some years later, when her eldest son Robert, married now to Vanessa with a baby of his own and living in a flat in the centre of London, went for a few days' late skiing holiday to France with his wife, and asked whether his parents would be prepared to come and stay in town and look after the baby.

Ruth was delighted to do so. A week in town! Just she and John – the idea was a delightful one.

It was Robert and Vanessa's second wedding anniversary on the day after their return and Robert, unknown to Vanessa, had ordered a cake from a small Italian bakery in Orchard Street. He arranged that Ruth would collect it, and pushing the buggy – she went to collect the cake.

There were a few tables there in the back of the shop where coffee was served and, while at the counter paying for the cake, Ruth heard someone call her name. 'Ruth?' softly.

She turned and saw at a table quite near, Julie Pinkerton, older now but as handsome as ever. 'Julie!' she said and leaning over her, kissed her impulsively.

'Have you time for a coffee – and – is this yours?' asked Julie, looking at the sleeping baby.

Ruth put the buggy in a suitable position and sat down opposite Julie, ordering a coffee from the waitress who came up.

'My grandson,' she said proudly. 'My first grandchild, Charles. Is this pushchair all right there?' she asked, and the girl nodded.

'Until lunch time,' she smiled.

'We'll be gone by then,' Julie replied.

'He belongs to my son Robert and his wife – they live up here – and I'm babysitting for a week while they are skiing. But this is wonderful. What are you doing here?'

'I live nearby – I have a flat in Orchard Street – I come in here most days – they have the best coffee.'

Ruth noticed a touch of grey on the smooth black hair while the dark eyes glowed, and she looked what she was, a very handsome woman.

Julie smiled at the baby. 'He's beautiful, isn't he? You must be delighted with him.'

'We are,' Ruth said. 'But I can't tell you how pleased I am to see you again. I've often wondered how you were—' But knew that as an excuse it sounded lame.

'I've thought about you too, and your daughter – Alice, wasn't it? Quite grown up now.'

'Training to be a Home Economics teacher,' Ruth said.

'Well, she always wanted to cook, didn't she?'

'And how is your husband?'

'Very well,' Ruth said. 'Looking forward to his retirement.'

She remembered, 'And how is – Patrick?'

'Fancy you remembering!' Julie laughed. 'Yes, he's still around – things don't change much there.' She glanced at her watch. 'Look, I have an appointment in a quarter of an hour—'

'I know you left Selfridge's,' Ruth said. 'I asked after you one day, oh, years ago—'

'Yes, I have my own salon – I work from home. I couldn't bear to give up my old clients and do you know some of them came with me? They were quite a prestigious lot, so I held on to them, and now I work from home.' She turned impulsively.

'Why don't you come and see me – perhaps one day when you come up to see your son – you could have a facial. I'm not expensive, in fact, I wouldn't charge you – it would be for old time's sake.'

'Oh, I wouldn't hear of that,' Ruth said. 'But I'd love to come.'

Julie opened her diary. 'What about Tuesday the 11th? Come at eleven and we'll have a good chat.'

Ruth could hardly wait until the time came around for the visit to Julie's and, finding the block of flats, took the lift up to the third floor and knocked at the door of number eight.

It was a small flat but Ruth was enchanted with it. A living room, bedroom, bathroom and kitchen, with a small room where Julie saw her clients. There was a single high bed and a dressing table with all the accoutrements of a beauty salon, shelves filled with various creams and lotions and make-up, and electrical instruments for various treatments. But the walls were covered with beautiful pictures and artefacts.

The sitting room resembled an antique shop, with treasures from all over the world which Julie told her she had collected on her travels. As a single woman she had earned money and used it to see the world. Mexico, South America, India, Afghanistan and the treasures were all mementoes of those visits.

Plaster statues, paintings, oriental china, exquisite porcelain, a wonderful Chinese carved cabinet in which she kept all her private papers, a small Louis Quinze sofa, two Georgian armchairs, small tables from Africa and India, rugs from Iran; it was an enchanting room, and Ruth could have sat and looked at everything for as long as it took. She never minded waiting for a client to go if she got there early.

Then Julie would appear in her white coat and would lead her into the treatment room where she would lie relaxed as she never would have at home, with a white headscarf and a light blanket over her feet. Creams would be applied to her face, her eyebrows would be plucked and, after a while, Julie would leave her to rest for ten minutes, when Ruth would lie back – it was like being looked after as a child again. Back again to clean her face, Julie massaged, and talked. Of her life, and how she had come to London with her mother where they had taken a flat at a nominal rent in Orchard Street. After her mother's death she kept the flat on and travelled whenever she could.

She had a boyfriend, Patrick, a married man, had had him for years. She adored him and used to meet him in the park and they would go for a meal. His wife did not enjoy the best of health and he couldn't find it in his heart to leave her. He was a barrister – and Julie was quite content to let this situation go on for ever if need be.

Ruth so enjoyed these visits to town and had been doing so for the past few years. During that time her other son Geoff, had married, Alice had a good teaching job, and she and John were looking towards their retirement.

She loved listening to tales of Julie's clients, some of them titled ladies who had stayed with her after she set up on her own. Some had died over the years and once she had shown Ruth a beautiful tiara, which was being worn on her wedding day by a client who had been with her since she was a young girl. Daughter of an earl, she had started coming to Julie at her mother's instigation, and was one of Julie's most prestigious clients.

'I am to make her up on her wedding day,' Julie said proudly. 'And afterwards I am invited to the wedding at St Paul's, Knightsbridge.'

Ruth was always absorbed by these stories of Julie's, often thinking how different their lives had been. Both in their sixties now, she had lost a husband and moved while Julie was still in the flat, seeing her friend Patrick, but not so often now, for he was approaching seventy and walked with a stick.

Ruth reflected that Julie's life was not so unusual today when a lot of women lived alone and had man friends, unable to marry, or from choice staying single. It had always seemed strange to her, for she had lived such a conventional life, and she had envied Julie her ability to travel and see the world. She imagined their friendship was the attraction of opposites.

Now she was at Paddington and, joining the queue, she took a taxi to Orchard Street.

Julie opened the door, delighted to see her; they kissed and Julie led her into the little sitting room.

'Just five minutes, I want to hear about your move,' she said. 'Just a tick while I wash my hands.'

Back again, she listened as Ruth told her about Apple Tree Cottage and Little Astons, the move and how strange it was.

'Sounds delightful,' she said wistfully, 'although for my part, I don't think I could live in the country – I've always lived in town. And yet, you know, I came from Devon originally.'

She ceased massaging Ruth's face for a moment and stared down into the busy street below.

'Did you?' Ruth asked, surprised.

'A long, long time ago.' And Ruth wondered, not for the first time, about her early life.

Having cleansed her skin, Julie began to apply make-up: moisturiser, foundation, a touch of blusher on her cheek-bones, and finally a dusting of powder, which she brushed away with feather-like strokes.

She showed Ruth the lipsticks. 'Which one – this one is better for your outfit.'

'Oh, I never bother with that,' Ruth said, 'I always wear the same one and when it's gone buy another—'

'Naughty,' Julie said. 'You should buy a selection and have fun – you'd be surprised . . . anyway, come through when you're ready and we'll talk over our drink.'

Ruth went into the little sitting room and immersed herself in its ambience, never tiring of gazing at the wonderful collection. On a side table was a large ornate silver mirror on a stand, very heavily embossed, beneath it a red rose which it reflected. She was curious.

Julie came in with a tray of dry martinis and smoked salmon sandwiches which she put down on a table, handing a dry martini to Ruth.

'Good health,' she said, turning round towards the mirror.

'Oh.'

Julie sipped her martini. 'Well, the mirror, I found it in Dubai, or somewhere, I can't remember now, somewhere Arab – and—' She broke off and looked at Ruth. 'Do you remember my telling you about one of my oldest friends, Margaret?'

Ruth thought. 'She died, didn't she?'

'Yes, sadly, months ago, about the time when your John—'

'Yes, I remember now, that's probably why—'

'It's her birthday today.'

There seemed no answer to that.

'I was very close to her—'

'She was married to a millionaire, wasn't she?'

Julie didn't answer, but stared ahead, seeing nothing. 'She was lovely. We had known each other since I first came to London; she came to me all the time for her beauty treatments; I always used to get her ready for her wonderful evenings, Ascot, the theatre. Henley, shooting parties, you name it, she did them all. She also,' she reflected, 'introduced a lot of clients to me and greatly increased my business.'

'Did they have children?' Ruth asked.

'No. Never wanted them.'

She looked at Ruth and smiled. 'Here, have a sandwich – salmon fresh from Selfridges.'

Ruth took one.

'We used to sit and natter, and she would talk to me – tell me all her secrets.'

Ruth wondered what was coming next.

'She was a compulsive gambler,' Julie said simply. 'Spent thousands, lost thousands, and he never knew.'

'He had no idea?'

'Not in this world. It was her secret – and mine. Of course, she had plenty, that wasn't the problem – and he adored her, you know.'

She glanced at the rose. 'I miss her very much. Of course, life changed when she married Albert Stringer – Bertie she used to call him. Then our lives were quite different – I was a working girl, she was the wife of a very wealthy man.'

'And still she gambled?'

'It was a compulsion – she couldn't help herself – addiction of any kind is difficult to deal with – she couldn't give it up. After all, she didn't need the money, she had plenty.'

'Did she gamble before she married him?'

'Yes, but in a small way, horses, pools – I never had any inclination myself, so I didn't understand it. She lost huge amounts but it never worried her – her only worry was him finding out.'

'And he never did?'

She shook her head and held out the plate. 'Have the last one, I've finished. My next client is at two, so we've plenty of time. I'll make some coffee,' she said as she disappeared into the kitchen.

When she came back she sat down abruptly. 'I think why I'm telling you all this, is because Bertie, her husband, has taken to calling on me. He rings to see if I am free then calls round for a drink or coffee; we perhaps have a walk in the park. He is lost without her.'

Ruth thought she could guess what was coming. 'Do you like him?'

'Not a lot,' and Julie smiled. 'He's not my type. Not like my Patrick,' and her eyes had a faraway look.

'He asked me to dinner in his apartment, in Park Lane. I've been there before with Margaret, but not on my own. It was lovely. You can't imagine how wonderful that apartment is – not the furniture of course – the home is non-existent in that sense, but the rooms, and the ceilings, and the setting – and the view—' She looked around. 'I'd rather have my little flat any day.'

Ruth leaned over and patted her hand. 'Is this leading up to something?' And she smiled.

Julie laughed. 'I don't know . . . is it?'

'What does Patrick think about it? Did you tell him?'

'Yes, I've no secrets from Patrick. He worries about me, what will happen when he can't visit me any more. Twenty-five years we have been lovers. I can't believe it sometimes.'

'But that's not how you see Bertie, is it?'

'God, no! He couldn't be more different. Patrick is a gentleman.'

'And – Bertie?'

'No, I wouldn't say he was a gentleman. He is very generous – gives a lot of money to charity, he's kind. I feel sorry for him.'

'But that isn't enough, is it – is it, Julie?'

'He is lonely after Margaret's death—'

'But that's not your problem, unless you want it to be, is it?' Ruth asked. 'Do you enjoy his company – or is it just the bond between you because you were both so fond of Margaret?'

'Well, there is that.'

'Of course, he hates coming here – says he feels stultified, cramped, can't be doing with all the fal-lals as he calls it.'

'Then you are dealing with someone who isn't in the least like you, doesn't appreciate the beautiful things in life. I can't imagine anyone not appreciating all these lovely things . . . What is the Park Lane apartment like?'

'Huge. Absolutely splendid – in one sense. Of course, it was built for luxury, but Bertie isn't a bit like that. It's almost sparse – and Margaret had no idea in this world. She was not a homemaker in any sense – no pictures on the walls, basic sofas—'

Ruth was astonished. 'Well, there must be something there?'

'No, nothing. Television – enormous – several chairs—'

'Antique?'

'No, just chairs. Coffee tables, remember the room is vast.'

Ruth got the idea that she was considering what it would be like to live there. 'Well, you're just friends,' she said soothingly.

Julie frowned. 'Yes . . . but I think it's building up to more than that. He really seems to need my company.'

'Doesn't he have any friends, hadn't they mutual friends?'

'Several couples, I think – not close friends. He has one man friend he has known all his life, but he is unmarried – lives nearby, with a flat in Nice.'

Ruth privately thought Julie was out of her depth but since she had always lived and worked in London with wealthy clients, she must have seen a good deal of the uppercrust side of London life.

She wouldn't be concerned like this, Ruth reflected, unless she was involved in some way with making a decision. There was more to it than being the friend to a deceased friend's husband.

When she was ready to go, she stood and picked up her handbag. 'Well, I should just enjoy it all while you can – lovely to go to some of these expensive places. Julie, you don't have to go if you don't want to.'

Julie was frowning. 'I knew you'd say that – you are so practical. The thing is, Ruth, he has asked me to go for the weekend to Eastbourne where apparently he keeps a luxury apartment at the—'

Ruth drew her lips together. 'Yes, I can imagine,' she said. 'And will you go?'

'I don't like to refuse – he hates being on his own—'

'Then you must make up your mind,' Ruth said, feeling much more worldly wise than she had a right to be, considering her background. 'How old is he?'

Julie hesitated. 'I'm not sure, older than I am and older than Margaret of course.'

Ruth made for the door. 'Talking of weekends – would you like to come down to Little Astons one weekend – when you can find the time?'

At last Julie relaxed. 'I'd love to,' she said. 'We'll fix something up – end of June, beginning of July?'

'That would be lovely. Well, I'll be in touch,' and Ruth made her way towards the lift.

She found herself unable to concentrate on anything other than Julie's tales and, after lunch, found herself disinclined to shop.

I shall go home, she decided. Back to Apple Tree Cottage – it feels more like home now. Oh, if only John were there to natter things over with. She would have loved to discuss her morning session with Julie although he wasn't a man for women's tittle-tattle. She had never seen Julie so disoriented. She was always in charge of a situation.

She admitted to herself though that she didn't want her own personal picture of Julie and her life disturbed. She wanted everything to go on as it always had . . .

Chapter Four

On a fine Friday morning in June, Ruth went to have coffee with Janet Foster at Plum Tree Cottage. As she passed the little house next door she noticed that the blinds were still drawn, as they had been ever since she moved in. Perhaps they were away.

At Plum Tree Cottage the small lawn had been carefully cut by one of her boys, while Janet kept the little garden trim. She worked so hard, went out a lot, although Ruth had no idea where she went. She probably had a job somewhere. Well, she would soon know.

She knocked on the little door, with its highly polished brass knocker, and was soon answered.

Janet stood smiling, a very pretty woman, Ruth decided, with her cascade of brown curly hair.

'Come on in,' Janet said, leading Ruth through the small narrow hall. Inside, it was quite unlike Ruth's cottage, for Ruth had had the wall knocked down between the hall and the living room to give more space. Janet's house was more conventional: a narrow hall leading to the two downstairs rooms, and a kitchen which had been extended at sometime out into the garden.

'This is cosy,' she said warmly.

'We'll take our coffee outside, if you like. It's almost ready. Now, how are you settling in?'

'Well,' Ruth said slowly. 'It takes time, but I'm getting

there – I hope. It's sometimes strange being on my own now.'

Into Janet's fine brown eyes came a look of compassion. 'Are you—'

'Yes – a widow,' Ruth said, knowing what she was going to be asked. 'My husband died about eight months ago.'

'I'm sorry, where did you live before?'

'Cheltenham,' Ruth said.

'Oh, what a change! What made you come here?' She poured out the two china mugs of coffee and, putting them on a tray with some biscuits, led them outside to the garden. It was pretty and cottagey and they sat at a small iron table.

'Isn't this a lovely spot?' Ruth said. 'We are so lucky to be living here. John and I always planned to come to the Cotswolds when he retired – but well, he didn't make it. We didn't think of Little Astons, specifically, although we always liked it. It is not so busy, not so touristy as some of the other villages, is it?'

Janet smiled. 'No, although quite a lot goes on here, believe it or not. I was born here,' she said, sipping her coffee.

'Were you – oh, how lovely! So there is nothing you don't know about the place. I hope you can help me find something to do – I know no one here – well, except my solicitor, who lives in Little Astons, which is convenient. His practice is in Cheltenham, but he lives here.'

'Then you must mean Mr Chadwick,' Janet said.

'I'm sure you know everyone here,' and Ruth laughed. 'Very handy for me. What about you?' She looked at the younger woman. You have a son, haven't you?'

'Yes, two, David is twelve and he lives with me, and the elder one is at Birmingham University,' she added.

'Wonderful,' Ruth said. 'What does he want to do? What's he reading?'

'History and physics,' Janet said. 'It's all beyond me – way above my head.'

'Good for him.'
'Do you have children?'
'Yes, three – my daughter, Alice, and two sons, both now working abroad.'
'You must miss them,' Janet said. 'Do have a biscuit – they're from Coppins, the bakery, you can get wonderful teas there – scones and strawberry jam and clotted cream—'
'Really? Do you know, apart from the local corner shop I haven't even walked down to the main shops yet, but it's a pretty little village, isn't it?' She decided to take the plunge. 'Are you on your own?'
Janet faced her squarely. 'Yes, I'm divorced. My ex-husband is in Spain. We lived there for a time but, well, it was not my cup of tea. I wanted to come home, and brought the boys with me.'
There was no more to be said on that, then, Ruth decided. 'I expect you work – what do you do?'
Janet laughed, and put down her cup. 'Oh, I've lots of jobs! I like it better – it's more interesting than one plain old job. So you think you might want something to do then?'
'Oh, I'd go mad just sitting at home all day!' Ruth said.
Janet looked at her. What age would she be? English people were obsessed with age, not a bit like Spain, or even America where they took you for what you were and age seemed of little importance.
She would be about sixty, she imagined. What you would call a respectable woman. Educated, spoke beautifully; she was calm and very attractive, with her iron-grey hair cut quite stylishly – that must be Cheltenham, Janet thought, and not the local one in Little Astons, although old Luigi was a good cutter.
She also, Janet thought, was restful. Lovely grey eyes, and a firm mouth as if she was used to taking charge, but she was not bossy. She also, she decided, wore good shoes – and shoes were Janet's passion. She liked her slim pale

skirt and the black v-neck sweater, a single row of pearls and pearl stud earrings to complete the picture.

'I passed the house next door to me,' Ruth said. 'Does anyone live there?'

Janet poured more coffee and held out the plate of biscuits. 'Not at the moment – it's sad really. I'd better tell you – someone will at some point. Young couple, two children – she's left him for another man and he is devastated. He works in Stroud and I imagine that's where he's staying. He came to give me a key, otherwise that's the last I've seen of him.'

'Poor man. How old were the children?'

'About twelve and fourteen – girls.'

'Oh, dear,' Ruth sighed, then realised she was treading on delicate ground with this young woman who had a broken marriage behind her.

'Well, what goes on in Little Astons? Are there clubs one could join, societies?'

'Depends what you are interested in,' Janet said. 'On Tuesday afternoons there is a women's guild at the local village hall, although I don't think that would be your cup of tea, and the local library service van comes once a week – that's useful if you read. We have an excellent book shop on the corner of the High Street – you must have a walk round, see what you think.'

'And what are these many jobs you do?'

'Well, on Saturday mornings I go along to the nursing home where I do a stint as hairdresser – I used to be a hairdresser—'

'Oh!'

'They have some nice elderly women there and some of them can't get out easily. I get paid, by the way, it's not voluntary work. Although once a week, if I have time, I do pop in to see how they are, get them a bit of shopping, something like that, they're a nice bunch of people. I read to one old lady – she's ninety-three.'

'Goodness!'

'Then I do two days a week at Luigi's – Tuesday and Wednesday – he's the local hairdresser. He's Italian, of course. Came here after the war, so he's getting on a bit. Then I do half a day, usually Friday afternoon, at Gregory's; he's got an antique shop. Well, it isn't so much antiques as a second-hand shop and when he has his half day I work in the shop. That's where I am going today. We have a lovely antique shop here, though, really lovely things, but I'm not knowledgeable enough to work there, although I'd love to. It's full of the most beautiful furniture.'

'Really,' and Ruth with her eyes on Janet's face saw her dark eyes shine as she thought of the lovely things.

'Then, on Thursdays, I work up at the Manor for Lady Bankes, showing people around. The Manor is open to visitors on Thursdays and Fridays but someone else does Friday. What do you do?'

Ruth smiled. 'Well, I'm retired now but I was a teacher. Right up until I was sixty.'

Janet's mouth was open, although why she was surprised she didn't know. That's just what she looked like – a school teacher, and she nodded her head. 'I can imagine. How wonderful, you must be clever, then.'

'Not necessarily,' Ruth laughed, 'but I found it rewarding. I had time off when my children were young but I went back each time and stayed until I retired.'

'Well, you won't be wanting a menial job, then,' laughed Janet.

'What's a menial job?' smiled Ruth. 'To tell the truth, I longed for the peace and quiet of the country, that's why I chose a quieter village. My husband would have loved it. I love gardening and walking, I suppose being shut up for long periods at school I wanted to escape.'

'I was just thinking that at the local primary school they need people to help the little ones to read but—'

'It sounds selfish of me, but no. Not at the moment. I don't feel like teaching at all, especially little ones. I need a break.'

'Well, there is a painting class on Thursday evenings, and an art appreciation class but that's in Cheltenham—'

'Yes, I know that, but I'd like to put some roots down here.'

'There is an embroidery school, in nearby Burford – lots going on in Stowe – and of course you could always go back to Cheltenham for real shopping and the supermarket. I go in once a week and do my big shop. We have a chemist, a greengrocer, a small shop that delivers newspapers and sells cards to tourists, that kind of thing, no dry cleaners, a rather smart dress shop called Francesca – and she is awfully nice – everyone knows her as Fran. You'd like her—'

'Well, I think that's enough to be going on with,' smiled Ruth. 'You've been very kind.'

'You're easy to talk to,' Janet said, thinking she was like the mother she would have liked to have had, instead of her real mother. Dead now, and it was a relief to everyone. She had been so bitter and miserable when Janet's father died, and had never recovered. She and her brothers had had a hard life but they had all inherited their father's temperament, and bounced back when things went wrong.

'Tell me about the Manor,' Ruth said. 'Is it worth a visit?'

'Oh, I should say. You should see what Fenella has done with it since she married Tod—'

'Fenella?'

'Fenella – Lady Bankes. I went to school with her—'

'Oh—'

'She always used to say she'd marry a rich man and she did. Mind, I don't think he's that well off, and she works hard with the visitors. Opened it to the public for the first time after they married. They've got two little girls and he has a son from his first wife. She died young.'

'How sad. How did he meet Fenella?'

'He came to open a village fête – his wife had been dead for about three years. Of course, he's older than Fen – she

She had kept it polished and they always had the 'clock man' in to set it – he had come after she had settled in at Apple Tree Cottage. She looked at it with a baleful eye and knew she was going to get rid of it.

'Sorry, John,' she said. 'But you're not here to argue with me.' She found herself quite often talking out loud. Perhaps, she thought, I'm going a little mad, but decided she wasn't. She just disliked the grandfather clock – all grandfather clocks. Besides, there was no room for it in this house . . .

The next time she was out in the village, she would call in to the antique shop and ask the owner's advice.

On Saturday morning Janet walked along Notcutts Lane to the Greystones Nursing Home. It was a drizzly kind of morning but a day that promised to be fine later.

'Ah,' Mrs Woolsbridge said. 'I'm glad you are on time – four today – Mrs Lethbridge wants to see you about a new library book, and Miss Willis needs a wash and blow-dry, Mrs Bligh wants to see you and Mrs Bancroft, because her daughter is coming to see her on Sunday, and she wants to look especially nice.'

'Oh, right, Mrs Woolsbridge,' Janet said, going to the cupboard and slipping out of her shoes and into flats, putting on her white coat and getting down to business.

She went first to see old Mrs Lethbridge. One of the nurses usually shampooed her hair, what there was of it, poor old thing. It was too late to offer her a new hair style, she thought, making her way up to the second floor. She was the only one up there because she never went downstairs.

'Now, how are we today?' she asked her. 'Did you finish the last book?'

'Yes, I did, Janet,' said Mrs Lethbridge proudly. 'It was lovely. Do you think you could get another one by the same author – whatever her name is?'

'Oh, I'm sure I can. I'll call in at the van – they have

quite a selection in large print. But, I keep telling you, you might like an audiotape, you could—'

'No, I don't like any of those newfangled things,' Mrs Lethbridge said. 'Just get me the book - dear, two if you can.'

'Will do,' Janet said. 'I brought you some mints—'

'Oh, you are kind,' Mrs Lethbridge said, taking the bag of mints in her gnarled old hand. 'You're a good girl, Janet.'

Janet found the old library book and, making sure the old lady was comfortable, left to go downstairs to Miss Willis, who was in no better mood than she had been last time.

'Good morning, Miss Willis,' Janet said, receiving no reply. 'Shampoo, today, is it?'

'And a trim,' Miss Willis said primly.

'Very well,' Janet said, looking at the fine silky silvery hair, which hardly needed cutting. But Miss Willis was very fussy. It must not be allowed to grow a mere half-inch before it was cut off close to her head.

Shepherding her back from the bowl, with a thick towel around her head, Janet smiled across at the elderly woman, receiving none in return. Janet watched her in the mirror and thought she hardly liked to see herself; it was almost as if she was ashamed of her looks, yet she wasn't a bad-looking woman.

As she rubbed the towel gently, for the hair hardly needed towelling, she began to snip with her fine scissors. It took no time at all, and when she had finished, she took off the cape, then smiled at her. 'How is that?' she asked. 'Will that do? Is it enough?'

Miss Willis glanced at herself. 'Yes, that'll do,' she said crossly.

'We won't use the drier then,' Janet said. 'I know you don't like it—'

'No, I don't,' Miss Willis said. It was almost dry anyway.

'Bye bye then, see you next week,' and she was out of there in no time – oh, what an old misery she was.

Next Mrs Bancroft, who she found in a state of great excitement because her daughter was coming to see her on Sunday. Excitement, not from joy, but trepidation, for she seemed to live in awe of her daughter, who was rather an exalted young woman with a powerful job in advertising.

'Now, Janet,' Mrs Bancroft said. 'Nothing fancy, but a nice set.'

'I brought you some moisturiser.'

Mrs Bancroft frowned. 'What?'

'Don't worry, it's just a beneficial moisture to put on your skin to keep it nice and soft.'

'It seems too soft to me as it is,' Mrs Bancroft said. 'When I think how firm it used to be—'

'Well, this will make it even firmer,' Janet soothed her. 'You've got a good skin – you should look after it.'

She shampooed her hair and followed it with conditioner then set it on rollers and used the drier gently to dry it.

'So your daughter is coming,' she said. 'That's good – it's a long time since you've seen her, isn't it?'

'Yes, must be March sometime – perhaps.'

'Now, what are you going to wear? Haven't bought yourself a new dress, I'll bet.'

'No, I don't need new clothes,' Mrs Bancroft said. 'I've got a wardrobe full but I tell you what, Janet, I'd be awfully glad if you would find something suitable, something nice for me to wear.'

'Well now,' Janet said cheerfully. 'Blue's your colour, have you got something blue?'

'Yes, I think I have.'

'Right, we'll get you going then.' And Janet, humming a little tune, went to the wardrobe.

She found a blue dress with small white spots and a white collar and a narrow belt. 'Oh, this is lovely,' she cried. 'Just you, and you've got some white beads.'

'No, I'll wear my pearls,' Mrs Bancroft said. 'They were my husband's wedding present to me.' She fingered them, seeing them in the mirror.

'And you've had them all this time,' Janet said.

'Janet, why don't you have a cup of coffee with me,' Mrs Bancroft said. 'The kettle's over there, it's only instant—'

Janet glanced at her watch. 'Well, okay, thank you.'

'Plug the kettle in, dear. You can make it.'

Sitting with her coffee in the other easy chair, Janet surveyed the room. 'This is the best room here,' she said, 'but then that's because you've made it so, with your own furniture.'

'Oh, I had to bring my things,' Mrs Bancroft said. 'After all, that's all you've got left, isn't it, when everyone—'

'Yes, and it's lovely ... You've a son as well, haven't you?'

'Yes, but he lives in Scotland – we came from there originally.'

Janet stared hard at the walls, at the pictures and the framed tapestries. 'Did you do those?'

'Yes, I did a lot of needlework when I was younger and had my eyesight.'

'They're most attractive,' Janet said.

'But no one wants things like that now,' Mrs Bancroft said. 'Mini something, isn't it called nowadays?'

'Minimilism – oh, that's only a flash in the pan,' Janet said knowledgeably. 'It'll pass – antiques and lovely things last for ever and so they should.' She stared hard at a little painting; it was so beautifully executed.

'That is particularly striking,' she said. 'I've often noticed it and thought – what an artist—'

Mrs Bancroft turned to her. 'Do you know who did it?'

'No.'

'Well, no matter. My husband was very keen on it. He bought that as a young man – it was his favourite picture.'

'Is it very old?'

Mrs Bancroft smiled to herself. 'Yes, I would say it most certainly is.'

'Well, it's really beautiful.' Janet sighed as she took her cup and saucer over to the tray. 'I'll wash these – have you finished?'

'Yes, thank you, my dear.'

'Then I must be off – and don't forget to put that pink lipstick on – your daughter will think you look like the cat's whiskers. Now, are you sure there is nothing more I can do for you – anything you need for next time?'

'Not that I can think of – thank you, dear.'

'I'll be off then – see you next week. Have a good time with your daughter.'

The last one – Mrs Bligh – and what would she be up to today?

Mrs Bligh was as excited as she could be. She needed a hairdo – and did Janet think a tad more red in the rinse?

'No,' Janet said. 'It looks fine just as it is. Now, where are you off to?'

'My friend, Mrs Lockerbie of the King's Arms, is picking me up at two and we're going for a drive – well, to Cirencester – we're going out to tea, and going to the shops. I desperately need some new clothes but I'm wearing my white skirt and my floral blouse – with the loose sleeves – and my very special necklace Joe bought for me.'

'Oh, that one,' Janet said, rinsing her hair and putting conditioner on.

'Is it cold out – do I need a jacket, or my Gucci scarf, what do you think?'

'I think it's going to be a warm afternoon – just your scarf, I expect, see what it's like.'

She stood back later and watched Mrs Bligh insert her long jewelled drop earrings which reached almost to her shoulders, her neck being so short.

She shook her head slightly from side to side. 'Oh, that feels better,' she said. 'I miss them when I haven't got them on.'

'Shall I get your blouse and skirt out for you?'
'Oh, would you? Please, dear.'
'This one?'
The white skirt was duly hung on the doorknob and Janet had some difficulty finding the blouse – there were so many and so many colours. But the cream, red, blue and green, with the frilled sleeves looked right.
'This one?'
'That's right, dear,' Mrs Bligh said.
'Well, I must fly,' Janet said. 'Have a good afternoon.'
'Thank you, dear. You too,' Mrs Bligh added.

Ruth was relaxing with a glass of wine after going to the garden centre to buy her summer flowering plants when the telephone rang.
'Ruth Durling.'
'Ruth dear, it's me, Julie.'
'Julie!' She was surprised. Julie hardly ever rang her at home.
'Ruth, would it be convenient for me to come and spend next weekend with you? Are you doing anything?'
'No, my dear. That would be lovely.'
'Well, I'll come by train probably in time for a spot of lunch – perhaps we could go to a local pub?'
'That's possible.'
'And stay overnight? Will that be all right? I will have to leave Sunday morning because—'
'Because?'
'Well, Bertie wants to take me to lunch on Sunday at the Connaught and I've promised to be back by twelve.'
'Goodness!' Ruth hoped the slight exasperation in her voice didn't come across to Julie.
'Now you're sure?'
'Yes, of course I am. I shall love to see you. Just ring me with the time of the train and I'll be at the station to pick you up.'
'You sure?'

'Yes, I'm looking forward to it.'

And she was, she thought, as she put down the phone. She was.

Chapter Six

By mid week, Ruth had quite made up her mind. The long-case clock must go.

She made herself some coffee then made tracks for the High Street, noticing as always that the blinds were still drawn in the house next door. She couldn't help but feel sympathy for a family so broken up although she had never met them.

She glanced in at the hairdressing salon which seemed to be busy and walked on until she came to MARTIN AMESBURY – ANTIQUES.

She could see a man at the far end of the showroom, no doubt Martin Amesbury himself, and then saw a notice at the side of the door. PLEASE RING. This she did, having tried the door, which didn't budge, and presently he came towards her, a tall, well-built man with thick iron-grey hair and very blue eyes, which she had to admit, showed no sign of welcome.

She heard the door click, and then it was open, and he stood there, as if waiting for her to speak.

'Good morning, are you open?' and she smiled pleasantly. 'Or have I picked the wrong day?'

He opened the door wide to allow her in. 'Yes, we are open. The locked door is a safety measure – these days—'

'Yes, I understand.'

He wasn't going to help her out.

'I wonder if I could have a word with you about a grandfather clock I have.'

He gave her no encouragement at all.

She smiled again. 'I have recently moved here, to Little Astons, and the clock I have – it is an old family relic – would you be interested—'

'You want a clock repairer?'

She frowned. 'No.' She spoke patiently. 'I want to get rid of it, I mean, I should like to sell it. Could it go perhaps to auction?'

'Possibly,' he said. 'What age is it?'

'I'm afraid I don't know – it belonged to my husband's family – and I really have no room for it in my small cottage . . . would . . . or could it go for auction? I understand grandfather clocks are—'

'Longcase clocks,' he amended, which sent her quivering inside with irritation.

'And you have no idea of its age?'

'Georgian, I would think,' and he gave a small smile inferring he had met many people like herself who thought they knew a thing or two about antiques.

He walked down to his desk, and she followed him, looking about her. He really did have some lovely things, but that didn't give him the right to behave so churlishly. She wished now she hadn't come in. He came back with a notebook.

'Could I have your name?' He looked out over her head to the street.

'Mrs Durling,' she said haughtily. 'And I live at Apple Tree Cottage, in Notcutts Lane.'

'Yes, I know it,' he said, closing his book. 'Would tomorrow be convenient – or Friday morning?'

'Tomorrow would be better,' she said, 'I am expecting—'

'Eleven?' he said.

'I'll see you then,' she said, and head held high, walked out of the shop and heard the latch click behind her.

She was furious. What a rude man! If he wasn't

interested why didn't he say so? Oh, she wished she had never gone near his ridiculous shop and, breathing heavily, she didn't simmer down until she reached home. She helped herself to a glass of wine with her lunch and afterwards found herself polishing everything in the room, especially the gr– longcase clock.

He was on time, she would say that for him, and thought what a fine figure of a man he was – perhaps because it was unusual to see a man walking up the path to her door.

'Mrs Durling?' he said, and she wanted to say well, who do you think I am? But decided to keep her cool and be as polite as she could in face of such hostility. Perhaps, she thought, he hopes to find a bargain – well, if he thinks that – I should get another opinion.

'This is it?' he was saying, quite politely, for after all, it stood in what had been the hall. He could hardly miss it. Then he turned blue eyes to her with the merest flicker of amusement.

She felt at a loss. Something had gone wrong.

Now he looked quite serious. 'I am afraid Mrs Durling, it is not quite what you think. I am sorry to tell you it is a copy – a Victorian copy.'

She was so cross she could have hit him. John's beloved clock! How dare he? She turned a cold face to him. 'A copy?'

'A great many of these were made in the Victorian era, I am afraid, copies of eighteenth-century workmanship – the wood is good – mahogany, and you have looked after it very well.'

Condescending so and so, she thought.

'I daresay it keeps excellent time.'

Don't patronise me, she thought, and gave him a stiff smile.

'Oh, well, whatever. Yes, it is disappointing, but there you are. I still haven't room for it, whatever it is. Could I put it into auction?'

He had mellowed slightly. 'Yes, I am sure – there is quite a demand for them, people want so-called antiques for their homes and will pay quite a good price.'

'I'm not interested in the money, I need the space.'

'Yes,' he agreed. 'A little large for Apple Tree Cottage.'

The way he said it made her think he knew the cottage. 'Do you know this house?' she asked.

'Yes, I've been here before, also,' he said slowly, 'my grandparents lived here.'

'He wasn't the old gentleman who laid out the garden?'

'I expect so – he died some years ago. Well, Mrs Durling, I'm sorry to disappoint you – not quite for me—'

Not good enough for you, she thought, that's what you are saying. She couldn't think when she had been so cross. Not at his rejection of the clock, but at his attitude.

'Well,' she smiled brightly. 'Thank you for coming – I'm sorry to have dragged you out.'

'Not at all,' he said politely and then his eye fell on a small prie-dieu in the corner, and she could see his eyes light up.

'Good morning, Mr er – Amesbury,' she said.

'Good morning, Mrs Durling.'

She closed the door softly and quietly to show she was not in a temper, which she was.

But mainly, she thought, for John. He had loved that clock. A copy indeed! Well, it didn't matter now – he would never know. She almost felt more fond of it than she had before. No, it would have to go. No wonder it was large, the Victorians always overdid things, and she had never taken much notice of it when it stood in the big hall at Montpellier.

She patted it. 'Don't you worry,' she said. 'You don't want to end up in his old shop.' And she wondered, not for the first time, if she really was going a little bonkers. Talking to oneself – wasn't that the first sign?

Julie rang her the next day to give her the time of the train arrival, and on Saturday, having prepared lunch rather than go out to a pub, Ruth set off for the station. She planned, with Julie's approval, to take her for a run this afternoon and for an evening meal. There was an excellent small restaurant in Little Astons which Janet had told her was very good.

She sat in the car outside the station, and after ten minutes' delay, the train pulled in.

It seemed so strange to see Julie out of context. She looked wonderful, with her upright walk, and her almost Spanish appearance, her very dark hair pulled back, and a three-quarter-length black coat over what looked like a black and white dress.

Ruth could have wept to see her, knowing they would be emotional tears – the sight of her old friend bringing back nostalgic memories. Somehow she seemed out of place in the country – not just because of her outfit, but simply because she looked like a city lady.

She jumped out of the car and hugged her. 'Oh Julie, it is good to see you!'

'You, too – and the air is so fresh after London,' and she breathed deeply.

'Yes, it is good, isn't it?'

'You're looking well – better than when I saw you in town last.'

'Well, I'm getting used to it now – it was strange at first, and after all, it's not long—'

'Since John died.' Julie said, clasping her seat belt on.

'It's not far to Little Astons, a pleasant drive,' Ruth said, starting up the car.

'Oh, it is so pretty!' Julie exclaimed as they drove along. 'Look at that little house over there – just like in a fairy tale.'

'Probably with no running water and no bath,' laughed Ruth.

'Really?' Julie turned serious eyes to her.

'No, I'm joking. Someone from town would have bought

it, then set about working on it – you should see some of them – absolutely beautiful, and they cost an arm and a leg.'

She turned into the High Street.

'This is our High Street – no Marks and Spencer, no Waitrose, but the shops are all right for run-of-the-mill things. Cheltenham is the place to go for a big shop up.'

'I remember Cheltenham,' Julie said. 'I once went there with Patrick, when we were younger, to a Festival, would it be?'

'Yes, I expect so,' and Ruth turned into Notcutts Lane, towards the row of cottages, past the large nursing home on her right, then stopped in the drive of Apple Tree Cottage.

'Oh, it's sweet!' Julie cried. 'Trust you to buy something like this!'

'It is nice, isn't it?' Ruth said smugly.

'Yes. It's lovely but don't you feel – buried? After two weeks I'd want to go home.'

Ruth laughed. 'No, remember I've never lived in London while you've spent a lifetime there.'

'True.'

Ruth was unlocking the door and led the way inside. The atmosphere was cosy and even indoors smelled as fresh as if it were still outside.

'Now drop your case, we'll take it upstairs in a moment. This is the downstairs cloakroom, yes, a loo and running water – I had that put in. So if you want to freshen up?'

'Please.'

Ruth busied herself at the lunch table, warming the French bread, courtesy of Coppins, until Julie returned.

'Now – for upstairs,' she said. 'There are three bedrooms.'

'Doesn't look big enough for that,' Julie said, 'but how nice, and you've done it all beautifully. Just like *House and Garden*.'

'Well, I hope you will find it a bit more homely than that,' laughed Ruth, 'and this is yours.'

It was a little room but big enough, with lots of yellow and tassels and the prettiest bedcover and matching curtains. An old French dressing table stood under the window and there was an easy chair and a cupboard for her clothes. There was also a washbasin set in one wall, which Ruth had insisted on because there was only one bathroom.

Julie was enchanted, and put her case down, going over to the window. 'Oh, it's the prettiest place,' she said. 'And the view—' she turned to Ruth with serious eyes. 'I hope you will be very happy here,' she said. 'It's not going to be easy.'

'No – but although we needed a smaller house as we got older, if I'd stayed in Cheltenham I would have expected John to be round every corner – here, well, I am trying to make a new life. Anyway, when you come down, we'll have a glass of wine and some lunch.'

They were half way through lunch when she asked the question she was dying to ask.

'And how is – Bertie?'

Now Julie looked serious. 'Oh, I've so much to tell you,' she said. 'Things have grown out of all proportion since I saw you last.'

Ruth looked concerned. 'What do you mean?'

'Well, things between Bertie and me have come to a head, if I can put it that way.'

Ruth kept silent and waited for her to go on.

'He seriously wants to marry me,' Julie said and Ruth's heart missed a beat.

'And how do you feel about that?' she asked, pouring more wine.

'Well, I never contemplated such a thing. A friend's husband – I never really knew him that well – it's all cropped up in the last few months. 'We talked and it seems he is quite serious. He is prepared to settle – this sounds awful – but he is after all, a multi-millionaire—'

'What?'

'A million pounds – apart from what I would get as his wife—'

'Sort of buying you,' Ruth said.

Julie frowned. 'That doesn't sound like you.'

'Sorry.'

'You're shocked, aren't you?'

'Well, let's say I can't understand how you've become involved with such a man.'

'You're making him out to be a monster but he isn't. He is very nice, rich, friendly, a man who is lonely without his wife.'

'So why does he need to bribe you?'

'Oh, darling, it isn't bribery!'

'What is it then?'

'Well, an inducement if you like, a dowry – you see, he says it helps him in a tax sense. But, you know me, I don't understand the ins and outs of the game on that level but, apparently, he makes a lot of money and, although he gives a lot to charity, he would like to have his wife back, so that they could enjoy old age in peace.'

'But you're not Margaret—'

Julie sighed. 'Well, I suppose he thinks I am the next best thing.'

'What does Patrick say? Or haven't you told him the real story?'

'Yes, I have. He thinks it might be a good idea, and he would feel someone was taking care of me in old age.'

'You're not old yet.'

'Yes, but I don't want to go into old age on my own – and neither does Bertie.'

Ruth had no idea what to say.

'Of course, there are provisos, conditions . . .'

Ruth raised startled eyes. 'Provisos? What sort of provisos?'

'I must give up my flat, and my business – he hates that little flat of mine – and, of course, he certainly wouldn't want me to see any of my usual clients.'

'So your whole life would change – the life you've always known?'

'But isn't that what happens when you marry someone? You adopt a new life – shared, with—'

'Do you realise what you'd be giving up? Your freedom – your marvellous business which you have built up yourself – how old is he?'

'I don't know,' Julie said thoughtfully, 'seventy something, I should think.'

'He's an old man compared to you.'

'I can see you don't like the idea,' Julie said. 'Well, I suppose I didn't think you would.'

Ruth went to put the coffee on. 'Do you like him?' she asked.

'Yes . . .' but she is doubtful, Ruth thought. 'I like him because he was my friend's husband and we have to have something in common.'

'But she was an inveterate gambler and you didn't have that in common.'

'Oh, Ruth! I shouldn't have told you all this. I knew you wouldn't like it.'

'I don't like to see you doing something you might be sorry for. At his age you could be his nurse, his housekeeper, his cook, his . . .'

'Darling, he has enough money to pay for all those.'

'When you talk together, do you have a lot in common?'

'Well, not really, our lives have always been so different. I've always worked for my living, I suppose you could say he has, but in a different way – in the lap of luxury.'

'Is he kind to you? Thoughtful?'

'Kind? What sort of question is that?'

'Oh, never mind. Polite, kind.'

'Well, as I think I told you before, he's not Patrick.'

Really, Ruth felt, she wasn't qualified to give any opinion as a distant friend of this woman. They had nothing in common – just a liking for each other. But she felt most keenly that she wanted her to stay as happy as she had always been – and wanted nothing to change that. Perhaps he would make her happy. It was not her business. Julie had obviously wanted to discuss the matter with her. But was Ruth qualified to give her opinion?

'You would be giving up your freedom,' she said at length.

Julie sat and thought for a long time. 'You miss John, don't you?'

'Yes, but I lived with John since I was, well, twenty-two.'

'Well, I've never lived with a man so perhaps now I am getting on is a good time to try.'

Something told Ruth she was not going to be put off. Deep down, she wanted this marriage – for whatever reason.

Then again – what attracted him to Julie? She was not of his world, she imagined, more sophisticated. Of course, she was good looking, he would be proud to be with her.

'We'll talk about it later,' she smiled. 'Let's just clear these dishes, we're going for a little drive.'

Never, she thought, have I wanted John so much. To be able to discuss things with him, get his point of view. He had been so level headed, so sensible . . .

Chapter Seven

After Julie had gone, Ruth spent a lot of time on Sunday evening dwelling on Julie's problem. That was the way *she* saw it – but perhaps Julie saw it as a hopeful future?

Well, there was nothing she could do about it. Julie must make up her own mind.

She looked in her notebook, and discovered that Janet probably had a free morning on Monday and Friday but more than likely she would have filled them in with something. She looked around – she really must get immersed in something apart from gardening for there was little to do in Apple Tree Cottage at the moment. Everything was new and in pristine condition.

Sometimes she drove herself around to tea or coffee in one of the villages to reacquaint herself, for she and John had done much driving in the Cotswolds. But when it came to something to keep her busy, she had no idea where to start. She would ask Janet – she was a mine of information.

Janet came in for coffee on Friday morning. Seeing her again, Ruth was reminded what a pretty woman she was, with that mass of curly dark hair and there was something about her expression that endeared people to her. She was a warm person; how her husband ever let her go, she couldn't think. But Janet never talked about him.

Ruth found she had a lot in common with this younger woman, despite the age difference.

'Oh, I do envy you!' Janet said when she came in, 'having such a spick and span house! Mine could do with redecorating – still, I'll get down to it when Ralph is home in the holidays.'

'Ralph?'

'My elder boy—'

'Oh, the one at Birmingham – I'd forgotten.'

'Look, I brought you some cherries from the supermarket,' Janet said. 'It's wonderful to see them now almost all the year round – used to be such a short season.'

'Oh, thank you but you shouldn't have – let me—'

'No, it's a small housewarming gift,' Janet laughed, laying the basket down on the kitchen table. 'I'm green with envy about your kitchen, mine's one of the old-fashioned ones. I did quite a lot when I moved in but then the money ran out and you know I could only modernise it a little. New cooker, and a fridge and freezer – I've yet to acquire a dishwasher.'

'It'll come,' Ruth said. 'Let's take our coffee outside – we have to make the most of this weather – heaven knows when it will suddenly come to an end and the skies open—'

'Too right,' Janet agreed, carrying the tray for her while Ruth carried a plate of scones and biscuits.

They sat in the garden, admiring Ruth's tubs of geraniums and petunias. 'And look at your apple trees!' Janet cried. 'They are laden with fruit and we've had the June drop, so they are doing well.'

'I don't know them all – I know one is a James Grieve, we had it at Cheltenham, and I think one is a russet – can't tell yet.'

She was dying to ask Janet about the old man who had lived there – if he was Martin Amesbury's grandfather or another old man. But she decided not to mention him, not yet anyway.

'Well, what have you been doing with yourself?' Janet asked.

'I went to Astons Manor on Friday,' Ruth said.

'Oh, and what did you think of it?'

'It was lovely – I was thrilled with it all. And –' she stressed, 'I went in to tea – and saw her ladyship—'

'You didn't! She came in, did she?'

'Yes, all in pink, well, a pale pink trouser suit—'

'I can imagine!'

'And she was so pretty! So gracious!' Ruth said.

'Yes, she would be,' Janet said, but not unkindly.

Ruth handed her the plate of scones, a small plate, jam, cream and a napkin.

'Might as well indulge,' she said. 'They were too good to miss.'

'Super,' Janet said. 'I can never resist them, although I try – have to watch my weight.'

'You don't seem to have a problem,' Ruth said, looking at the slim figure in her black trousers and cream top.

'Not up to now but I did get quite plump when I was in Spain – still, it soon wore off when I came home.'

'I'm dying to hear more of the story of the couple up at the manor,' Ruth said. 'After all, it's very romantic, isn't it?'

'Yes . . . I suppose it is. It was the talk of the village for a long time.'

Ruth poured more coffee. 'Did you really go to school with her?'

'Yes, we were neighbours, we were friends – lived in the same street, Wool Yard, just behind the church.'

'What an extraordinary name. Is that real?'

'Wool Yard? Well, there are lots of connections with wool, the Cotswolds being one of the centres of the wool industry, so I suppose it follows.'

'Oh, I've a lot to learn,' Ruth said. 'Anyway go on.'

'We were kids together, went to the same school, liked the same boys – you know how it is. We used to see the boys at church on a Sunday. Francesca, you know, who owns the dress shop, was our Sunday school teacher – well, she was only a few years older than us. We used to talk and make plans, what we could do with our lives and Fen – you know Fenella – always said she was going to marry a man with lots of money and move away to London and have a big house. She was a real romantic – waiting for her prince to come!

'Well,' and she drew a deep breath. 'When we were sixteen, she fell in love with Eden Brook – mind you, I'm not surprised – he was so handsome, tall and fair, we were all a bit in love with him, but he fell for her too.

'He'd just come to live in the village – his father bought the tailor and outfitters on Crisp Street. Eden and Fen used to meet whenever they could, but her mother tried to put a stop to it. She was so ambitious for Fen – she knew she was beautiful and wanted her to make a good marriage – well, what chance did she have in a country village?

'Anyway, Fen and Eden were together for about two years, when I met Jack, my husband. I married at twenty. Jack was a hairdresser in Stroud, and I trained there, and well, to cut a long story short, I married him, and we lived in Stroud over the shop and the boys were born there.'

Ruth poured more coffee.

'After I was married I still came back to see my mother and bring the babies, and used to see Fen, still going with Eden – she told me once they were going to run away and get married when she was twenty-one. But Eden didn't want to leave his father alone – his mother had died, and his father hoped he would take over the business.

'It was all a bit sad, for Fen, really. Her mother was absolutely adamant. Over my dead body, she used to say when Fen said she would marry Eden.'

'Oh, how sad,' Ruth murmured. 'Then what happened?'

'One day when I came home to see my mother the village was agog with gossip. As I told you, there had been a village fête – Lord Bankes had met Fen, his wife had already died – well, briefly that was that.'

'But what about Eden?'

She shrugged. 'He's still around. Never married. His

father is dead, and he runs the shop. Fen had two little girls, helped to put the manor back on its feet. His lordship is as happy as a sandboy, presumably.'

'But do you never talk to her these days? After she married?'

She shrugged. 'Never see her. Of course, I volunteered for the job up at the manor, because I was back from Spain by then, and frankly I needed the work, and I was curious but another woman trained us, and I rarely saw Fen – it was as if we had never been close friends. Funny really.

'There is a lot of gossip in a village, Ruth,' she said after a while, brushing herself down from crumbs. 'You will find that out. Nothing's sacred. I don't mean in a malicious way – but whatever is going on, someone hears about it, and whoops, it's out. It's amazing really how fast news gets around. One woman moved away because she found that news in a village travels too fast but it never bothers me – I'm used to it. Brought up to it. It's harmless prattle – you can't keep a secret, I tell you,' and she laughed.

'Well, a village like this is one big family, I suppose,' Ruth conceded. 'I've never lived in a village so it will be a new experience.'

She could see that Janet was getting ready to go. 'While we're on the subject of the village – I wondered if you had any more thoughts about what I might do with my time? Come the winter months I'm going to need something to do.'

'What would you do if you lived in Cheltenham on your own?'

'Well . . .' and she hesitated. 'You see – it's less than a year – and I was busy selling the house, and seeing to everything, then looking for a property round here, so I was fully occupied. It's only now that I realise that I hadn't thought it through but it would be the same wherever I went.'

'Well, if you had stayed in Cheltenham, you would have found lots to do. I expect it's bursting at the seams with ideas – societies, clubs, that sort of thing.'

'True, but—'

'You didn't want to stay in Cheltenham,' Janet smiled. 'There is a Red Cross circle here. I think they meet once a week and sew – at any rate, they need funds – that might be useful.'

'Sounds possible,' Ruth said. 'Where are the headquarters?'

Janet laughed. 'Nothing as elaborate as that, I'm afraid. They meet at Doreen Lister's house, once a week, or fortnight – I'm not sure. Shall I mention it to her?'

'Oh, if you would,' said Ruth. 'That's a start, anyway.'

'Something may come to me. I'm addleheaded at the moment,' Janet said. 'I've heard, between you and me, that Luigi, the hairdresser, is selling up next year and, as I mentioned to you, it is my dearest wish to buy him out. Of course, money's the problem. Still you never know, so I'm keeping my fingers crossed.'

'Oh, that would be wonderful,' Ruth said. 'But does that mean you wouldn't be able to see the ladies at the nursing home?'

'Yes, a bit of a problem – still, we'll sort something out. I would hate to let them down. Perhaps *you* could meet them sometime – Mrs Bancroft, Mrs Bligh and Miss Willis?'

'Miss Willis?' Ruth queried.

'Yes, poor old soul, she is such a misery – I wish I could do something for her.'

'What is she like – Miss Willis?' asked Ruth.

'To look at, you mean? Well, thin, very short hair, I think she used to be a teacher. Well, I must fly – that was really lovely Ruth, I am glad you came to live here!'

Ruth closed the door after her. She sat down thoughtfully back in the garden. Miss Willis . . .

A Miss Willis had taught in the school at Cheltenham where she had been. A tall, grey lady, Miss Willis and Miss Dobson. They were inseparable. Miss Dobson was short and pretty and plump – and coy – Ruth could see her now. She wore a lot of rouge on her cheeks and lipstick and pretty dresses, while Miss Willis – could not have been more different.

They lived together in a small house a mile or so away from the school, shared a car – it was accepted that they were lesbians. These days it was discussed more openly.

Ruth had heard that Miss Dobson had died suddenly after a stroke eighteen months ago, and that Miss Willis had moved into a home. Was this the same Miss Willis?

She rather thought so. How bereft she must be. No wonder she hardly spoke – nothing could console her for the loss of her great friend and companion.

A bit like her missing John – what was the difference? Lovers or husband and wife – you had to feel pity for a broken partnership.

A few days later she made up her mind. She was always grumbling that she had nothing to do. Going into the High Street she called at the florists, where she bought a sheaf of mauve and pink lilies. Well, if Miss Willis refused to see her, she would take them home.

It was very impressive, she thought, the entrance to Greystones Nursing Home and, having pressed the bell, she waited. A young woman came to the door and, when she said she would like to see Miss Willis, she looked totally shocked.

'I'd better get Mrs Woolsbridge,' she said, hurrying off.

Mrs Woolsbridge soon appeared, suspicion written all over her face.

'Yes?' she said.

'Is it possible to see Miss Willis?' Ruth asked.

'Miss Willis!' Mrs Woolsbridge said. 'I'm afraid she doesn't see visitors.'

'But I have brought her some flowers and she might agree to see me,' Ruth said. 'She will know who I am.'

'I doubt it.'

'Mrs Durling, she'll know who I am. I am a friend.'

'Go upstairs to Miss Willis's room, Kate, and tell her there is a Mrs Durling to see her. Come inside,' she said.

Once inside, Ruth glanced around her. The place smelled of disinfectant, and a not unpleasant smell of some kind of room fragrance.

Kate came down the stairs. 'She said to go up, Mrs Woolsbridge.'

'Very well,' still no answering smile from Mrs Woolsbridge. 'Up the stairs, first room on the right, number 6.'

'Thank you,' Ruth said, and went up slowly.

Tapping on the door she waited.

When she saw her her first thought was – oh, how she has aged! She looked so old, so thin, poor Miss Willis; and at first Miss Willis didn't know what to do. Then she saw the flowers, and her face seemed to crumple.

'Oh, Ruth,' she said. 'How nice of you to come—'

Ruth smiled broadly. 'Hello, Edith,' she said.

Chapter Eight

Ruth was really pleased with her visit to Edith Willis. Poor woman - how strange it must feel, retirement, after a lifetime of teaching, her beloved friend gone - no wonder she was depressed.

But they had talked over old times. Edith had no idea Ruth's husband had died and they had teaching and the school in common.

If word was said, she would merely tell Janet that they had taught at the same school. She didn't think it necessary to go into details about Edith's life. Edith was a very private person, and from things she had said about her sons Janet seemed rather straight-laced. Though Ruth hoped she was wrong, she had an inkling that she wouldn't be quite so tolerant of Edith's past relationship.

Be that as it may, she was glad she had seen Edith Willis, who after a time had relaxed, and even laughed once or twice over old times. She wasn't a bad old sort, really. She was older than Ruth, having retired at sixty-five.

Well, now, she thought, a visit to Doreen Lister, whoever she was, who lived very near the church in the centre of the village, which was very convenient. She found herself using her car less and less these days, as she seemed to live on top of most things.

She passed the antique shop, but there was no one in view; there was never a time when she passed it that she didn't recall the rudeness of Martin Amesbury. But she wouldn't think about that now.

The Byeway was a little row of cottages, with tiny front gardens, spilling over with flowers in pots and baskets and window boxes. Number four belonged to Doreen Lister, although whether she was single or not, Ruth had no idea. She had telephoned her first before arranging to call on her.

The door was opened by a small woman who looked competent enough to be in charge of anything – the Army or the Women's Institute. She oozed self-confidence, her brown eyes twinkling a welcome to Ruth; a bright smile and sturdy legs led the way into the tiny sitting room.

'Well, my dear, it is good to see you. We need more help these days than we ever did. Such a lot of trouble in the world and it is up to us to do what we can? Eh? Sit you down – anywhere.'

Ruth subsided gratefully into a high-backed chair: she had an idea that you didn't slump when Mrs, or Miss, Lister was about.

'By the way,' she said. 'I am a widow and I understand you are too.'

'Yes, but a recent widow,' Ruth said. 'I'm still coming to terms with it—'

'Ah, takes a time,' she said. 'Now, I am sure you could do with a cup of tea. I'm just going to make one.'

'That would be nice,' Ruth said and, when Mrs Lister disappeared into the kitchen, she looked around the tiny room. The cushions were embroidered, and there were embroidered pictures on the walls, plates which had been hand painted – such a colourful room – and full of a woman's artistry, which Ruth appreciated.

'Now, my dear,' Mrs Lister said, 'and you must call me Dolly – everyone does – short for Doreen – I never felt like a Doreen,' and the fine teeth flashed in a smile. Her face was wrinkled like a walnut but it didn't detract in the least from her charm.

'Now, you are offering to help us,' Dolly said, when

they were taking tea. 'You know what we do? Janet told you?'

'Well, not really. She said you aim to raise money for the Red Cross – in various ways, making blankets, toys, that sort of thing.'

'Yes, in many ways. We have fêtes, fairs, all kinds of things. We meet on a Wednesday afternoon – here, as a rule, although we take turns, if convenient, and sew or knit. At the moment, we are knitting squares for blankets, which we sew together but you might know all about that, I daresay. Janet told me you used to teach in Cheltenham.'

'Yes.'

'We send the blankets to the Red Cross for anywhere where there is trouble – there's always a war somewhere, but we have almost finished this one and we are going on to something else.'

She handed Ruth a plate of biscuits. 'We are having a fête in July, and of course, we have our own stall. We shall be selling bric-à-brac: homemade cakes, if anyone feels like making one and they are always popular, jewellery, anything that we think is saleable. I hope you can make that – 29 July, and you could begin by collecting as much stuff for the stall as you can. In the meantime we meet here on Wednesdays at two-thirty – can you manage that? Not a bad day for you?'

'Not at all,' Ruth smiled.

'How are you liking Little Astons? Notcutts Lane, isn't it?'

'Yes, Apple Tree Cottage,' Ruth said.

'Know it well – a charming place. We knew the old man who lived there. And another thing – we do have a choir on Friday evenings – does that interest you?'

'Can't sing a note, I'm afraid,' Ruth said ruefully.

'Oh. Pity, still there's lots to do here – you see, while the young ones work, it's up to us oldies.' She looked at Ruth approvingly. 'Now if you get any ideas for fund raising, do let us know – we're always glad of ideas. We put on a play at Christmas – the local children you know.'

'Oh, that's nice.' Privately she thought, I don't want to work with children just at the moment, I need a break, but still, so far, so good.

She stood up. 'Well, thank you for the tea, Dolly,' she said, as Dolly beamed.

'I'll see you out,' and she opened the small front door to allow Ruth to escape to the outside world.

'Well,' her daughter Alice said when she telephoned that evening. 'What have you been up to?'

'Not a lot,' Ruth said. 'I've joined the Red Cross—'

'What?'

'The Red Cross – it's a group of women who work to raise money for the Red Cross.'

'Oh, I thought for a moment you were going out to Iraq.'

'God forbid . . . No, I'm gradually finding my feet.'

'Good,' Alice said, matter-of-fact as always. 'Well, see you soon, take care.'

She presented herself at Dolly Lister's on the following Wednesday afternoon, and was shown as before into the small sitting room. Three women were grouped round a card table, which was filled with large baskets of coloured wool and needles, while folded up on a chair was a multi-coloured blanket.

Two of them looked up and smiled, while the other one nodded briefly.

'Now, ladies, we must welcome Ruth Durling,' Dolly said. 'She has come to join our group. This is Betty Harrison.'

Betty lifted her eyes. 'Hello,' she said in such a small affected voice that Ruth quite lost interest, 'Olive Measham.' 'Hello there,' Olive said in a deep voice, 'welcome to our little group,' and Dolly said, 'Mary, Mary Lavender.' Mary gave Ruth a huge smile and Ruth took to her at once.

She was a tall, well-built woman with a crop of grey curly hair and a long face, but a face that showed warmth and greeting.

'Mary used to be the publican's wife at The Swan,' Dolly informed her.

'For my sins,' Mary said. 'We hear you've just moved in to Apple Tree Cottage. It's a dear little house, with such a lovely garden.'

Now was the time to ask about the old man but she was cut short by Dolly rapping on the table sharply.

'We'll have finished that last strip today,' she said, 'and I think we ought to discuss the fête.'

There was a tap on the door, and a young woman entered with a tea tray.

'Ah, thank you, Emma,' she said, 'you can put it down. This is our new member, Mrs Durling – Emma comes to give me a hand on Wednesdays,' she said, as Emma went out closing the door behind her.

She poured the tea and handed it round. 'Now, I'm going to make a list of things we shall require for the fête. Can I count on anyone for a homemade cake?'

They all said yes except Ruth who had a sudden brainwave. Why – Alice. She would surely make a cake, if she had time, that is, so she raised her hand with the others.

'Now, apart from the usual bric-à-brac, have we got enough left over from the Christmas Fair?'

'We gave it to the Girl Guide jumble,' Mary said.

'Oh, so we did. Well, we shall have to start from scratch. Anyone got any ideas?'

'What about handmade toys?'

'Oh, children don't want those things today. All those lovely little stuffed and knitted things we used to make, they only want computer games and that sort of thing.'

'Not the babies,' said Betty.

'Oh, well, if anyone wants to make a few toys, we won't refuse them.'

'Bunches of cut flowers?'

'Now how long would they last if it was a hot day?'

'Produce from the garden then, fruit?'

'Yes, except that we don't want to tread on old George's stall – he sells only fruit and veg.'

'I still think china and bits and bobs sell the best – people are always looking out for a bargain,' Mary said.

'Has everyone got plenty of bric-à-brac?' Dolly asked.

'I'm sure we can rake up enough for a stall.'

'What about you, Ruth?' Dolly asked.

'Oh, I am sure I can rake some things together, moving house is always a good time to sort things out.'

'We'll leave it at that, then. Now, we will have finished the blanket, I'll sew it together this evening, but what next?'

'Sewing?' Olive asked. 'I prefer it myself.'

'What do you mean, like a patchwork quilt to raffle?'

'Yes, that's always fun and it brought in quite a bit last time.'

'Then that's settled,' Dolly said. 'We shall want all your spare bits of material, remember, so don't throw anything away.'

Ruth walked home, pleased with her afternoon, but it hadn't been quite what she meant. She wanted to learn, to acquire knowledge, there must be some evening classes where she could polish up her French perhaps, or art appreciation classes? What about a book group? And all the things she had never had time for when she was working? Something would turn up.

She had just turned the corner into Notcutts Lane when she saw the SOLD board outside the house next door. What a surprise. But she was not surprised when half an hour later Janet knocked at the door.

She entered swiftly. 'What do you know!' she said. 'I had no idea!'

'That's a well-kept secret then,' smiled Ruth.

'I didn't even know it was on the market. News like that gets around very quickly as a rule.'

'Perhaps it was sold privately.'

'Yes, oh, well,' Janet sighed. 'Now you will have a new neighbour. Notcutts Lane was due for some changes. But I must get back – Ralph is coming home this weekend and bringing a girl.'

'Oh.' Ruth smiled. 'Is this the first time?' Janet was frowning. 'You don't like the idea.'

'Well, I suppose there is always a first time – but you know, he's not yet nineteen and has got his college work to do.'

'Oh, Janet. He needs a break.'

'Anyway, I've told him. No monkey business. He must respect my house – or there will be no more entertaining girls. He can sleep with David and the girl can have David's room.'

Ruth was looking at her.

'What?'

'Nothing.'

'You do agree with me?'

'Yes, this sleeping-together lark is a bit much for me but you hear of it so often. It wasn't the way mine were brought up but that was then.'

'This is now and believe me – things haven't changed,' Janet said.

And Ruth knew that Janet wished young Ralph had never asked the girl home.

She sighed. Oh, she was glad she didn't have to go through that stage any more.

Later she telephoned Alice.

'Alice, could I ask you to do something for me?'

Alice sounded apprehensive. 'What is it?'

'Could you make a cake for the Red Cross fête, it is for charity?'

'Yes, sure. I'll get the girls to do it,' she said. 'Good practice for them. Everything all right? Good, take care – bye.'

*

How her life had changed, Ruth thought. In less than a year. She had lost her husband, moved house, become part of a rural community, made some new friends – you never knew what was round the corner.

And then the telephone rang.

'Ruth?'

'Yes – Julie, is it?'

'Yes,' and she sounded excited.

'Listen – are you free next Thursday – the twelfth?'

'Yes. I am sure I am.'

'Would you be free to come up to town?'

'Up to town?'

'Yes. Bertie would like to meet you.'

Oh! She hadn't expected that.

'And afterwards, I would like to take you to lunch at the Ritz.'

'The Ritz? Whatever for?'

'Well ... it's a sort of celebration – just the two of us. I'll explain when I see you. Come here first and we'll take a taxi to Park Lane. Is that all right?'

'Yes, sure,' Ruth said, and had the awful feeling that she wouldn't like what Julie was going to tell her.

Chapter Nine

Towards the end of the week, Julie telephoned, saying there had been a slight change of plans.

'Lady Adair is coming at ten and I don't want to let her down, so would you go straight to Bertie's Park Lane apartment about eleven o'clock, then we'll have coffee, and afterwards proceed to the Ritz for a drink in the hotel followed by lunch.'

She gave Ruth the precise address and Wednesday found Ruth catching a train in plenty of time to reach Paddington and thence to Park Lane.

She had dressed carefully for the occasion, in a cream tussore silk suit and brown top, an outfit she had had for a long time but kept for special occasions, and being a classic cut, it never dated. She had originally had it made for a wedding.

Her shoes had high heels, were brown, matching her crocodile handbag, a present from John, old now, but as good as new.

She had had her hair done, at Luigi's of all places, and was very pleased with the result. Just a wash and blow dry. She might experiment with the cut later.

And of course, the pearls that John had bought her . . .

She felt curious as she sat in the train and not a little apprehensive and, as the train reached its destination, thought – well, what's the worst that can happen?

And it was that Julie would marry this man, this Bertie – and then wish that she hadn't?

Perhaps it was the best thing in the world. A thing that Ruth should be very happy about for her friend. The opportunity to marry a millionaire. That didn't come to many women – except that today it was more probable than it ever had been. But she couldn't shake off the doubts, the trouble she could foresee. Was she becoming a misery as she got older? Older people were often notorious for looking on the black side of things, perhaps because they had a short future. But, firstly, she wasn't like that – and she was certainly not old. Since she had lived at Little Astons she had not felt her age – and she was lucky, she knew. You had to make the best of it – otherwise things could happen – events, like John having a heart attack before the age of sixty-five. Morbidity, she thought, buck up, Ruth – you are going to see a dear friend.

At Paddington she had to queue for a taxi. Things had changed a great deal over the past few years, since the station was undergoing refurbishment, if that's what they called it. It was a nightmare travelling anywhere, crowds of people looking lost, staring up at the departure boards, which often did not forecast their train, at least not the one they wanted . . .

When her turn eventually came, she was pleased she had allowed enough time for all these problems, which had meant getting up almost at dawn – the taxi pulled out into Praed Street and made its way towards Hyde Park, which seemed to be, as it always was, thronged with tourists. In Park Lane the coaches were parked one behind the other, and as the taxi passed by the end of Oxford Street, she could see the place thronged with visitors, shops, newsvendors – that didn't change.

The taxi pulled up about half way down, before the Dorchester, and she found to her pleasure that Julie was waiting outside for her, looking so smart – dressed entirely in black with a white top, somehow looking strangely unEnglish, well dressed beside all these tourists or visitors in their jeans and sweatshirts.

Julie hugged her, her dark eyes alight with excitement.

'You haven't been waiting long?'

'No darling – just a few minutes.' Taking Ruth's arm she led her past the commissionaire who stood at the grand entrance and into the most enormous foyer, with its marble floor and great urns of flowers on marble stands, to the lift gates embossed in gilt.

'Second floor,' Julie said pressing the button. 'Soon be there.'

Another soft-carpeted wide corridor with each heavy carved door leading to its own apartment and there were only two of these. There was no sound in this sumptuous place of the road and noise of London traffic below.

The door was opened by a stout woman in a white overall, who almost bowed to Julie.

'Norah, this is my friend, Mrs Durling, we'll go straight through.' And Ruth wondered why Julie didn't have a key.

In the small inside hall, Julie took off her jacket. 'Do you want to keep yours on?' she asked.

'Please,' Ruth said, and Julie, glancing at herself in the mirror, took them through to a vast drawing room, which appeared almost empty because of its lack of furniture and ornaments or pictures.

The room itself was impressive, could hardly be otherwise, because of its size, but that was all. Two great chandeliers hung from the ceiling, the only sign of ostentation, one large picture (a reproduction, Ruth noted), and three sofas, modern and not of good quality. Four armchairs, a low coffee table – a magnificent fireplace, all this she took in at a glance before seeing the large chair at the end of the room in which sat an elderly man.

Julie walked towards him. 'Bertie,' she said; his chair swivelled round, and she bent and kissed him lightly.

'This is my friend Ruth, Ruth Durling.'

He didn't smile, perhaps wasn't a man who smiled

easily; he put down the paper he was reading and held out his hand.

'Excuse my not getting to my feet,' and he gave a small smile. 'My gout is bad today.'

Ruth saw that his foot was resting on a stool. 'I'm sorry,' she said, looking at him and trying to assess what she saw. White hair, quite thick, blue eyes, rapier sharp, beetling brows, a quite handsome face.

'Sit down, dear,' Julie said, pushing a deep chair a little nearer. 'I'll go and see to the coffee.'

'Black,' Bertie called after her.

'Please,' Ruth muttered under her breath, and told herself to be open minded. She was too quick to judge - she wasn't at school now.

'And you live in—'

'The Cotswolds,' Ruth smiled, 'in a village called Little Astons.' He said nothing. 'I moved there after my husband died nearly a year ago.'

'What did your husband do?'

'He was at the Foreign Office,' Ruth said, a closed look coming to her face. Over the years, she had a special look for anyone who enquired about the work that John did.

'I see. Do you play the stock market - shares?'

'Of course she doesn't,' Julie said, coming back into the room. 'On its way,' she said.

The woman who opened the door stood the tray down on a table, and poured.

'How would you like it, madam?' she asked Ruth.

'Black, please,' Ruth said and after pouring it the woman walked off.

There were no biscuits - perhaps, Ruth thought, because they were going out to lunch later.

Julie smiled across at Bertie. 'Ruth lives in the Cotswolds, in a little village called—'

'Yes, she told me,' he said shortly.

His hands were beautifully kept and Ruth sat trying to guess his age. She was sure he was older than Julie had suggested. But what was it to do with her? It was thoughtful of Julie to ask her to come up to town and meet him.

'Did you know my wife?' he asked. 'Margaret?'

'No, I didn't,' Ruth answered, deciding to keep her answers short and sweet.

'Ruth never lived in London,' Julie said, giving Ruth a smile. 'She's a country lass.'

'Wonderful woman,' he said, and Ruth saw a cloud pass over Julie's face.

'Yes, she was,' she said.

'I'm giving a ward to the Nesbit Children's Hospital in her memory – they are going to call it after her.'

Glancing at Julie, Ruth saw her face almost crumple, until she regained her composure.

'Very generous,' Ruth interposed.

He glanced at her, then at Julie. 'Where are you going today?' he frowned.

'The Ritz,' Julie said. 'To lunch.'

'What have I got?' he asked, rather like a spoiled child, Ruth thought.

'Salmon, darling,' Julie said. 'You could have come.'

'No thanks,' he said shortly, and Ruth felt she had been dismissed.

'More coffee?' Julie asked her.

'No thanks, that was fine.'

'Well, I'll show you around the flat, then we'll go.'

She kissed the top of Bertie's head, and led Ruth through to the great dining room, impressive in its size, but a long table seating twelve and a sideboard was all it contained – and a cocktail cabinet circa 1930. The bedroom held twin beds and was quite austere; a second bedroom; a third; while Bertie's study was filled with files, papers, books – all leatherbound, a huge desk and it overlooked the park.

'What a wonderful room,' Ruth said.

'Well, that's where he spends almost all his time – making money,' Julie whispered, laughing. 'Not a room I am allowed in, thank goodness.' She closed the door softly and they returned to the drawing room.

'Well, we'll be off now, darling,' she said.

Ruth held out her hand. 'Goodbye,' and then remembered she didn't really know his name, but he did hers.

'Goodbye Mrs Durling,' he said, and opened up his paper again.

They made for the entrance. 'Well, that's that. I'm glad you've met him - could I have a taxi, please,' she said to the commissionaire.

'Certainly, madam,' and he whistled in the way that porters have, and a cab stopped almost immediately.

'Lot to be said for this life,' Julie hissed in Ruth's ear.

In the taxi, she turned to Ruth. 'Well, what do you think?'

'What a question!' Ruth answered, playing for time.

In no time they were outside the Ritz Hotel, and then inside.

Ruth, who remembered it from a special anniversary she and John had spent there, thought it hadn't changed all that much - except for the people.

They went towards the small anteroom where, being shown a table, Julie asked for two dry martinis.

Ruth was fascinated - it was all so far removed from her life in Little Astons. She saw one or two familiar faces - an MP, a famous actor and sat back to enjoy herself. What a change from the Cotswolds! Here you felt in the centre of everything, and she sipped her dry martini with pleasure.

Julie leaned forward. 'What did you think of him - Bertie?'

'What a question!' Ruth played for time. 'I only saw him for five minutes—'

'Oh, you know what I mean,' Julie said. 'Impressive, isn't he?'

'He's that all right,' Ruth agreed. How could she really say what she meant? That she thought this marriage would be a disaster and she didn't know why.

'Well,' and Julie put down her glass. 'I've decided. I'm going to marry him.' She waited for Ruth's reaction.

Ruth was not surprised at her words, for she was quite genuinely horrified – but she couldn't put it into words without hurting Julie.

'Well,' she said slowly. 'The decision is yours, isn't it? It has nothing to do with anyone else.'

Julie's face fell. 'That's tantamount to saying you disapprove. But why?'

Ruth thought. 'Well, I don't quite know why you are doing it, except for the money—'

'Oh no! Not at all – but is that such a bad reason?'

'Look, dear Julie, it's not my business. Remember, your life has been quite different from mine – how would I know what is good for you or not? I'm thinking of marriage per se – you know, not a marriage between two people who have lived totally different lives. It's such a big step at this stage . . .'

'You're worried I won't make it?'

'More worried that he won't,' Ruth said grimly. 'He was devoted to his first wife – are you being asked to fill her shoes? Because, obviously from what you've said, that would be impossible. She sounds quite a different sort of woman. I see you as a generous person, kind, loving, caring.'

Julie was silent. 'I value your advice, Ruth,' she said eventually. 'You are one of the most true friends I have. Most of my friends are my clients but you – I don't know, you're something special.'

'Bless you,' said Ruth, 'and you are very special to me. I've known you a long time – not well – but a long time. I only wonder, will he make you happy or are you giving everything to him? What is he giving to you – apart from the money?'

Julie took a deep breath. 'He will give me security in my old age—'

'Oh, come on now,' Ruth said.

'I mean it. The chance of a full life – with money behind me – who can argue with it?'

'Well, I can, for one,' Ruth said. 'Are you sure you are not going to turn into a nursemaid, a housekeeper, who is the woman – Norah – is she staying on?'

'Yes.'

'So the household will be run by her. What will your job be?'

'To keep him happy, look after him, see that things run smoothly, and for this he is going to settle a great deal of money on me, Ruth.'

'I don't like that part,' Ruth said. 'It denigrates you. It's tempting, I can see that but – what are you going to get out of it, apart from the money?'

'Companionship, company,' Julie said.

What on earth could they have in common, Ruth wondered . . .

'Do you get on together? I'll say it again – is he kind to you?' She had not seen much evidence of that while she was there.

'Of course he is.'

'Does he seem fond of you?' It seemed to her he had lived for his wife Margaret – what did he want out of it? Companionship? Well, you couldn't argue with that, two elderly people, although she suspected that Bertie was a lot older than he seemed to be.

'Anyway, doubts aside – I am going to marry him!' Julie said, her eyes shining. 'That's what this is about – we are celebrating. It is to be in September, quietly, no guests, at a register office, we don't want any fuss,' and Ruth felt suddenly fearful for something that was going to change both their lives. 'This is my wedding breakfast.'

'Well,' she said at length. 'I should congratulate you, I suppose. Sorry if I've been such a Job's comforter.'

'But, listen – you will be pleased. He wanted me to give up my dear little flat and my clients, but I have been promised it in writing that I may keep my flat, but not of course, the clients. That he wouldn't listen to. He doesn't like anything that will take me away from him, but my dear little flat will still be mine.'

'And you will have to give up your clients?'

'Yes, he simply would not listen to that. So, when you come up to town you can come and see me at the flat, and we'll have lunch as we used to but no more beauty treatments. I promised. I don't mind, it's time I retired. And I shall live at Park Lane. After all, that flat has been mine for thirty years, although I don't own it, but he is prepared to pay the rent for me – even buy it, he says.'

'Oh, well, that's good.'

The waiter brought the menus for them to study and, once they had chosen, came back to take their order.

'Will you like living in that great apartment?'

'I've told him it must be refurnished – after all, I couldn't live in that gloomy atmosphere – new furniture, that sort of thing – and he has gone along with it, but insisted that I don't fill it with my bric-à-brac. Well, as you know, I couldn't live without that, so I shall be able to use the flat when I like.'

If he lets you out of his sight, thought Ruth.

'Your table is ready, madam,' the waiter said and they walked into the beautiful dining room.

'Oh,' Ruth exclaimed. 'I have always thought this is the most beautiful dining room in England.'

The view over the park through the windows was magical on such a fine day and there was such an atmosphere – from the painted ceiling to the delicate and beautiful furnishings, the table settings . . .

'I could dine here every day,' Ruth said happily.

'One day we may be able to,' Julie grinned.

It was the money, Ruth decided. Did she know Julie all that well? She determined to make the most of it. It wasn't every day she dined at the Ritz.

'So tell me – when is the wedding to be? No guests at all? Does he have any relatives?'

'A few but none that he is close to,' Julie said.

'You know, I think you've got some pluck,' Ruth said. 'It's not everyone would take on an elderly man.'

'But I'm no longer young,' Julie said. 'I see it as a job I've applied for - a well-paid job - and I've got it.'

'What will you buy for the apartment?'

'Oh, some nice furniture - decent carpets, that sort of thing. But I'm not bothered about that. He's such a nice man, Ruth, really ...'

'I'm sure,' Ruth said, 'or you couldn't marry him.'

'That's why I asked you to dine - we are not having any guests, it is to be private - but I thought we would celebrate on our own, since you are such an old friend.'

The waiter came up with their first course.

While she waited for him to serve Julie, she looked around at the other diners; her eye was caught by a couple at the table on the opposite side of the room, and she gave a start.

'What is it?' Julie said.

'Nothing, just someone I thought I knew.'

But she did know her - if only by sight.

It was Fenella, Lady Bankes. Dining with a man of about her own age, a good-looking, fair-haired man who looked slightly familiar, although she couldn't place him.

They were engrossed with each other. Hands across the table ... She was mesmerised.

She wasn't mistaken. It was Fenella, Lady Bankes ...

'Bon appetit,' Julie said, raising her glass of wine.

Chapter Ten

'Alice,' Ruth said on the telephone a few nights later. 'You remember the grandfather clock – in the hall?'

'Yes, Daddy's clock?'

'Well, I really don't have room for it in this house and—'

'You're not going to get rid of it!'

'Well, it's just in the way – far too large for—'

'But I thought that was for me! Daddy always said—'

Thank goodness I didn't sell it! thought Ruth. 'Darling, if you can do with it, it takes up a lot of room—'

'Of course I want it. It's mine! Oh, I should love to have it!'

'Where will you put it?' Ruth thought of Alice's house crammed to the doors with the belongings of herself and husband and three children.

'Where will I put it? In the hall – wherever. Oh, that will be lovely!'

'Well, I will pay the transport charges so don't worry about that. Anytime you feel you can pick it up—'

'I know a good man here – he's used to carrying antiques.'

'Yes well, you make the arrangements, let me know and I'll settle the bill.'

'Everything all right with you?'

'Yes, fine, thank you, and you?'

'Yes, take care, bye.'

A week later the removal men arrived.

'Bit of a corker, isn't she?' the boss said, staggering under the weight.

Ruth smiled and nodded.

'They don't make them like this any more.'

'Indeed they don't,' Ruth said, closing the door after giving him a good tip as, swathed in hessian and blankets, it was carried down the drive.

Oh, what a difference it made. Now she had all the room in the world. A small table perhaps with a very large display of flowers – like up at Astons Manor.

Mind, there was a danger of knocking into it – a small, slim one then. Still, she felt she could breathe now. And what's more, John, she smiled, your beloved daughter has it, so everyone is happy. So much for the miserable man up the road and, humming to herself, she went in search of a small table in the spare room . . .

'Where's the clock?' Janet asked when she called in on Friday morning. This was in answer to the large board outside Cherry Tree Cottage, which proclaimed HARVEY AND COLEMAN – HOME IMPROVEMENTS.

'Haven't wasted much time, have they?' she said. 'I've no idea who's bought it – did you hear anything?'

'Not a word,' Ruth said. 'Come and sit down for a minute, I've got the kettle on for coffee.'

'That will be nice.' She leaned her chin on her hands. 'I must say, it looks heaps better now you've got rid of the clock – did Martin buy it?'

'No, he wasn't interested, but my daughter Alice was thrilled to bits. Always thought it as hers by rights, apparently.'

'Funny how they like the old things,' Janet said.

'By the way, your Martin whatever his name is – was a little offhand to say the least when he came to look at it.'

'When was that?' Janet asked.

'Oh, a month ago, I suppose.'

Janet was thoughtful. 'That would have been when—' and she stopped. 'Well, there's no harm in you knowing,' she went on. 'His wife Stella, left him.'

Ruth turned, open mouthed. 'Left him?'

'Yes, it would have been about a month or so ago. She was a so and so – a partner in the shop with him, so you can imagine how he misses her. Has to run it on his own, and that's no joke. By the time you've been out buying, and set the shop to rights, and then being in the shop and so on, it's too much for one person to handle.'

'What do you think the trouble was?' Ruth asked. After all, if she lived in the village, she might as well become au fait with whatever was going on, although she had it in her heart to feel little sympathy for him. Bad enough when a husband or wife died – but to walk out . . .

'I won't go into the details – it's not fair, but nobody liked her – behind his back she was – well, as I say. I think he's well rid of her. Still, he's lost a business partner as well as a wife.'

'Did they have children?' Always the first question in Ruth's mind.

'A daughter – lives in South Africa. She doesn't get on with her mother but she adores her father.

No accounting for tastes. Ruth found that hard to imagine. He had been so taciturn, still, there had been a reason.

She decided to change the subject. 'How did you get on that weekend when your son brought his girlfriend home?'

'You cannot believe. I need not have worried. He met her in Birmingham, at a party, she's due to go to Cambridge later this year, studying Astroph—'

'Astrophysics?'

'Astrophysics – yes, that's it. A proper brain box. Quiet, not even a diamond in her nose. Her hair scragged back but she did wear drop silver earrings – otherwise nothing. No make-up.'

Ruth had not met Ralph yet but from what Janet said, he sounded like a serious-minded young man.

'How did you get on at the Red Cross?'

'Oh, I'm going to make a cake, and I have to collect bric-à-brac, which you might drop in if you have any?'

Janet interrupted her. 'I know what I was going to say. You went to see Miss Willis.'

'Yes, I did.'

'How did you know who she was?'

'I used to work with a Miss Willis at Hetherley School, and I put two and two together, and thought, well, if it's not her, it doesn't matter. Someone will be glad of a few flowers.'

'Well,' Janet said. 'It did the trick. She actually spoke to me quite pleasantly. You quite cheered her up. That was kind of you, Ruth.'

'I enjoyed seeing her. She lost her oldest friend, you know, some time ago, and I expect she misses her.'

'Poor old thing, and by the way, my Mrs Bancroft hasn't been too well. She looked rotten when I went on Saturday morning. I hope that daughter of hers didn't upset her.'

She got up. 'Thanks for the coffee. I must fly - due at Gregory's at lunch time. Never a dull moment.'

Some of the shops in Little Astons still closed for lunch between one and two, shops that might not be affected by the tourist trade. Owen Brook, Tailor, was one of them.

Hurrying to her afternoon job at Gregory's, Janet remembered that David needed socks, and she had promised to get them. It was never any hardship to call in at Eden's shop, for she still had a soft spot for him even after all these years.

Making her way to Crisp Street, there was the neat little shop which sold everything for men. Socks, ties, shirts, pyjamas, hats - while in a small anteroom, upon shelves, were stacked bolts of men's suiting. It was surprising how many local people still went to Eden Brook for their handmade suits and sports wear.

The little bell rang over the shop door, and Eden came

through from the back, his fair hair still thick and unruly, his ready smile anxious to oblige.

'Hi, Janet.'

'Oh, Eden, I've just called in for some socks for David. He grows out of them faster than I can mend them.'

'Size?' Eden queried.

'Size nine shoe, I can never remember.'

'He likes the black ones, doesn't he? Is it for school?'

'Yes, navy or black.'

He laid them on the counter.

'Two pairs, no, better make it three.'

'And how are you keeping?' he asked her.

The close proximity of this man never failed to disturb her. He hadn't changed all that much and she often wondered why he had never married. It must have been an awful shock when Fenella ditched him to marry that lord of hers. Still, it was all old hat now but no one had ever seen him with anyone else. He lived the life of a village resident and was respected by everyone, carrying on the business much as his father had done.

'Going to the dance at the hall next Friday?' Janet asked.

'No, I'm going up to see my sister in Harrogate.'

'How is she?'

'Great, two kids now.'

'Oh, that's nice.'

He put the socks into a small paper bag and took her money, ringing up the till and giving her the change.

'I see Cherry Tree Cottage is sold – do you know—'

He shook his head. 'No, no idea. I didn't know it was up for sale.'

'None of us did,' Janet said. 'Oh, well, bye then, see you.'

'See you, Jan.' As the door closed behind her, he came over and shot the bolt.

Janet went on her way to Gregory's. What a waste of good manhood – surely he didn't still hanker after Fenella – that had been years ago.

She and Jack had been together ever since they were at school but the arrival of Owen Brook and his handsome young son had stirred up half the girls in the neighbourhood. If I hadn't been so mad about Jack, she thought now, I might have gone for him. Silly me, my life might have been quite different. For Eden Brook would have made a good husband, of that she was sure.

The door was open at Gregory's as usual and, going in, she was assailed by the usual smell of second-hand bits and bobs of furniture.

'Ah, there you are,' said Gregory from his hideaway. 'I am glad to see you, we've had a rush on this morning.'

'Well, I'm going to get cleaning,' Janet said. 'Smells stuffy in here.' She knew that to be the understatement of the year.

Well, wait until she got her hairdresser's shop – then she could do what she liked.

Ruth took a stroll around the village on Friday afternoon, buying some postcards of Little Astons to send to the boys, one in Dubai and one in Canada. She hoped that Robert might be home for a short time this summer – she was looking forward to seeing him so much.

Passing Martin Amesbury's antique shop, she saw out of the corner of her eye a dear little narrow table – just the thing for the hall and much more suitable than the one from the spare bedroom. Well, it would have to stay there, and she would manage with the one she had.

At the back of her mind was the thought that she would like to find Crisp Street and the little tailor's shop where the young man lived who had been her ladyship's first love.

After all, the man who had been with Fenella need not have been a local man at all but he *had* looked slightly familiar and she had no idea why.

Since that day she had made up her mind to ferret out the tailor's shop and see if she could identify the man who had been with Fenella Bankes, out of curiosity she had to admit and the fact that she wanted to piece things together.

After all, it was not for her to judge if Fenella met a man in London – he could have been her brother but she didn't think so. Or a business acquaintance but they had been too close for that.

No, she decided, Ruth, you have become a village person. You are doing this out of sheer nosiness. Be that as it may, Crisp Street, a narrow little street off the end of the High Street was soon located, and there it was: Owen Brook – Bespoke Tailor.

Well, there was nothing she needed in there, she wasn't likely to go in to buy anything, so she gazed idly in the window at the merchandise. Very smart, she thought. Quite expensive for a local village shop.

While she was looking a man emerged from inside the shop and went to a shelf, from where he took something down. He was tall, fair haired, good looking – and yes, it was the man dining at the Ritz with Fenella Bankes. Her heart missed a beat and she felt quite guilty.

Goodness – and she hurried on her way, as if she had been found out doing something she should not. Which is true, she thought, slowing down. What's the rush?

Janet had a quick peek at Cherry Tree Cottage on Saturday morning as she passed on her way to Greystones, but there was no sign of workmen around – no vans or cars.

She went through the usual procedure, giving the elderly lady upstairs her new library books, and stopping to have a chat with her before going in to Mrs Bancroft, who was lying back in her chair as if she was exhausted. She was twirling a hankie in her hand, crumpling it, and when Janet entered, she turned such weary eyes towards her that Janet knew she was not at all well.

She went over and took her hand. 'How are you?' She pressed her hand. 'A bit under the weather? Well, I can understand that – it is very warm out – close, takes it out of you.'

Mrs Bancroft sighed. She was pale and there were dark circles under her eyes.

'You're feeling all right, are you?' asked Janet. 'Did you see the doctor – did he come yesterday?'

'Yes, he did, such a nice man. He's put me on some special tablets – says I am depressed but I've never been depressed in my life.'

'Well, there is a first time for everything,' smiled Janet. 'Everyone gets depressed sometime or another in their lives – you'd be surprised.'

'Do they? I suppose I never had time.'

'Did you have a busy life?'

'Yes, I did. My husband ran an important printing business and I had to entertain – a busy social life – it doesn't seem possible now. I can't think where I found the energy—'

'That's because you're not feeling well,' Janet said. 'Now, I can see you won't feel like having your hair done today.'

Mrs Bancroft shuddered. 'Oh, no, my dear, let's leave it for a bit. Perhaps you could come in for me one day next week . . . see how I am, shall we?'

'Yes, sure,' Janet said. 'I tell you what I did buy – some chocolates – would you fancy those?'

'Oh, my dear, you are kind!' Mrs Bancroft said. 'Thank you so much.'

'How did the visit from your daughter go? I didn't ask you.'

'Oh, well, she didn't stay long – she's always busy you know, has a very exacting job—'

I'm sure, Janet thought.

'Now you're sure you'll be all right? I'll call in one day next week – see how you are. Try to have a sleep this afternoon. Oh, and here is a magazine – I don't know if it's to your taste but you can give it back to me when you've finished it.'

Mrs Bancroft took her hand and she pressed it. It was

frail like holding a wild bird and Janet shuddered inwardly. She didn't think Mrs Bancroft was long for this world. But, sometimes you could be surprised. She might pick up and be full of beans before you could say Jack Robinson.

These oldies were remarkable. She thought that even more when she knocked at Mrs Bligh's door, because Mrs Bligh was singing at the top of her voice, 'I will survive'. And when Janet was inside the room she could see Mrs Bligh had two hands on her skirt, as though she were dancing and her eyes were merry – and very much made up.

'Oh, Janet,' she said collapsing into a heap on the bed, quite breathless.

'Now, what have you been up to?' Janet asked. You couldn't help laughing at her. She wore a short tight skirt, which barely covered her knees, showing a pair of well-developed legs, and a blouse full of frills and masses of pearls and earrings.

'Oh, I've been waiting to see you – I want my hair touched up again today—'

'What – this morning?' Janet said.

'If you can, dear,' she said. 'I thought it was getting a bit dull, don't you think?'

'No, I think it's – lovely,' Janet said.

'Still dear, just a touch-up.'

'As you wish,' Janet said, rolling up her sleeves and going into the bathroom to get the mixture ready.

'You sure you've got time?'

'I'll make it,' Janet grinned. 'Well, did you enjoy your outing with your friend?'

'Oh, it was lovely,' Mrs Bligh said. 'We had a smashing lunch and guess what – I met a man—'

So that's it, thought Janet. That was the usual reason.

'He works at the Unicorn. Do you know it, dear?' but she didn't wait for Janet's answer. 'He's the under manager there,' and her eyes positively glowed.

'Of course, he's young,' she went on, as Janet spread the mixture over and into her hair. 'Nothing like a young man to keep you going, is there dear?' Her eyes looked positively wicked.

Janet stared into the mirror. Incredible when you think this woman and Mrs Bancroft were about the same age – and look at the difference. Luck of the draw, she decided.

'So, tell me, what's he like? Handsome?'

And Mrs Bligh began, 'Oh, you can say that again!'

Chapter Eleven

By the time September came around, Ruth had telephoned Julie at the flat in Orchard Street two or three times, but there was no reply. She had no number for the flat in Park Lane, and would not have telephoned if she had, respecting Julie's wishes that the marriage ceremony would remain their own affair.

The fête had come and gone and had been highly enjoyable. She was surprised at how many visitors turned up and altogether they made two hundred and fifteen pounds for the Red Cross Fund.

By now, workmen had arrived, about four of them at the house next door, and it seemed that it was really being refurbished.

Towards the end of the first week, she was surprised to see Martin Amesbury walking down the drive of the next-door cottage where he stood outside for some time watching the men at work, before going inside the house.

Well! Ruth sat back on her heels from gardening, where she was dead-heading the roses and snipping off the dead geraniums.

What was the meaning of that? Could he have – no, surely not.

She put the secateurs in the pocket of her gardening apron and went farther down the garden. She didn't want him to think she was prying but, presently, the sound of her door bell reached her half way down the garden.

She hurried back to the front door and opening it saw Martin Amesbury standing there.

She was horrified to find that her face had flamed and she felt quite warm. With temper, she assured herself. 'Good morning.'

'Good morning, Mrs Durling.'

She stared at him.

'May I come in?' he asked, quite affably.

'Yes, yes, of course,' and she stood back to allow him in. What was all this about?

As he came into the hall, he glanced to where the clock should have been but he said nothing.

She led him into the living room. 'Do sit down,' she said.

'I'm sorry to bother you,' he said, 'but I thought you should know that I have purchased the house next door – Cherry Tree Cottage—' and she nearly fell over with shock.

'Bought Cherry Tree Cottage?' she repeated.

'Yes, for investment,' he said. 'I really came to apologise for all the noise and so on that you must be having to put up with. I know workmen are the very devil when they get going and I'm sorry for any inconvenience you may be caused.'

Well, she thought what a turn around . . .

'I haven't been bothered as yet,' she said politely.

'They are half way through. I have had some drastic improvements made in the kitchen and bathroom and now there is the general decorating and the outside paintwork.'

'Yes, of course,' she murmured. Why was he telling her this? 'You are not going to live in it yourself, then?'

He smiled. 'Oh no – but I am quite fond of this little lane and when the opportunity came up to buy, I thought – well, why not? Investment in property is always a good idea, especially nowadays, the market seems fairly steady, at least, it doesn't look as if it is going to collapse.'

'Let us hope not,' she said.

'I understand there is a great demand for rented houses in the Cotswolds so, business not being all that great at the moment, I thought I would re-invest—'

Oh, she thought. That's an admission – business not being great. She still couldn't forgive him, but she was glad he came.

'Well, that's very kind of you,' she said. She wasn't going to offer him coffee. 'Thank you for coming.'

'You have done wonders with this house,' he said, looking round.

'Thank you,' Ruth said. 'It was worth it – it's a dear little house.'

He smiled. 'Yes, I have lovely memories of it . . . Well, I must be on my way.' Getting up he walked towards the front door.

'Where is the – er – clock?' he said. 'Did you manage to sell it?'

She froze again. 'No, I did not manage to sell it – my daughter has it – apparently she had always thought it should go to her – so she has it. I'm glad I didn't get rid of it—'

'Ah, children,' he said, as if they had that much in common.

'Well, thank you for coming.'

'I expect them to be finished in about three weeks, I hope so, then you will finish with the noise and the inconvenience.'

She smiled tightly. What an odd man. Falling over himself to be nice, she wouldn't wonder.

So, new next-door neighbours. Now, what would they be like?

The following week she had a telephone call from Julie.

'Ruth? Darling, I've been trying to get you for ages—'

'And I you,' Ruth said, 'but I only had the number at Dorset Street.'

'Well, I am not often there,' Julie said.

'So how are you?' Ruth asked.

'I'm fine and you are talking to Mrs Albert Stringer,' Julie said proudly.

'Oh, you are already married?'

'I did tell you September – two weeks ago.'

'I would like to have sent you some flowers,' Ruth said.

'Oh, no need for that! But I thought you'd like to know.'

'Of course! And are you happy?' Ruth asked.

'Very,' Julie said. 'It seems very strange at first – to be Mrs Something, and to be wearing a ring.'

Ruth laughed. 'When am I going to see you?'

'Not easy at the moment – just settling in.'

'Do you go to the flat much?'

'Not at the moment – I'm busy choosing stuff for the Park Lane flat and I have to do it on my own, Bertie has no interest. I have carte blanche and that's rather nice for a change.'

Ruth said she would imagine so.

'Well, we must keep in touch,' she said. 'Is Bertie well?'

'Yes, he keeps very well,' Julie said.

Did she imagine it or did Julie sound different?

By the beginning of October, the men working on the house next door had cleared away their rubbish and the skip outside had disappeared and two strong men had made a very good job of the garden.

Delivery vans began to arrive with furniture and then an upmarket interior-design-business van from Cheltenham arrived and spent two days in the house and tasteful curtains and blinds were installed.

Oh, very nice, thought Ruth. But with his business, Martin Amesbury would know what was what; she wondered why she still felt touchy about him. Possibly because he had downgraded John's gr– longcase clock and she couldn't forgive him for that, which was petty she knew. Nothing short of his coming to tell her he had been mistaken, and it really was a valuable antique could make her feel any different, and she laughed out loud at the thought.

Next came a prestigious removal van and men began to move furniture into the house. I must not stand here and stare, Ruth thought, even though she would dearly have loved to see what was being taken in.

Well, it would be good to have someone next door after an empty house for so long.

She busied herself in the back garden, pruning the roses and collecting the dead leaves, carrying them in the wheel-barrow down to the compost heap and the bonfire site. There was nothing like a good bonfire – she would look forward to that later in the year. In recent years they had not been allowed to have bonfires in suburban areas and she had missed that. She turned her attention to the fruit trees. It needed someone other than herself to see to those and she thought of the old man who worked at Greystones Nursing Home. Perhaps she would ask him.

It was getting quite dark now, the sun had gone down, and soon it would be time for putting the clocks back. She always hated that time; most people did. It seemed so unnatural. Then, suddenly, the back doors were opened of the house next door, and men were carrying chairs and tables outside into the garden and walking down the side path. She retreated quickly into the shed and put things away. She was so used to it now, it was like home. With new people next door, she really felt like an old resident.

With a last look round, she locked the shed door and the back garden door, saw that the van was still outside in the dusk, drew the curtains and went upstairs to take a bath.

'Well, John,' she spoke out loud, as she relaxed into the milky scented bath, 'I am going to have new neighbours – very exciting,' for sometimes his absence was unbearable and loneliness quite overtook her.

She lay reading for a long time that night, only putting her book down when she could hardly see to read.

She was up, though, bright and early, as she remembered the events of yesterday next door. She pulled back the curtains and, sure enough, the van and all signs of a removal had gone, only a black BMW stood in the drive, pristine, the sun glinting off its bonnet.

All was quiet at Cherry Tree Cottage.

Preparing her breakfast, she thought, I suppose I must go and call sometime to make them welcome but I'll leave it for a day or two, let them settle in. Although who they were she had no idea and reminded herself that they were tenants who were renting the house from Martin Amesbury and not the new owners.

Later that morning, she was dusting the sitting room when through the window she saw a woman coming down the path towards the front door, swinging a bunch of keys. She looked familiar.

Surely, she thought, surely, that is the dress-shop lady – elegant, her hair glinting in the sun, what was her name – Francesca, Francesca Anderson. She hurried to the door to answer the bell.

A smiling woman stood there, who held out her hand. 'We meet again, I am Francesca Anderson, you came into my shop—'

'Of course I remember,' Ruth said. 'Do come in.'

Francesca stepped inside. 'I am your new neighbour,' she smiled. 'I'm renting the house next door.'

Ruth, surprised, was not quite sure what to say. 'Well, welcome,' she said. 'Welcome to Notcutts Lane, except you probably know it better than I do. Do come in and sit down.'

Francesca followed Ruth into the hall. 'Oh, this is nice,' she said. 'You've made some changes.'

'Yes, quite a few.'

By now, there was a fire burning in the grate, a gas pretend fire, but it was warming, and gave a welcome, and Francesca looked around appreciatively.

'Well, I have to say you have made this very comfortable, you wouldn't think it was the same house,' she said. 'I hope you don't mind my calling on you?'

'Of course not,' Ruth said, drawing up a chair. 'I would have called anyway but you do surprise me – what are you doing here?'

'It's a bit of a long story,' Francesca said.

'Look, will you have coffee?' Ruth asked.

'Thank you, yes.'

Well . . . Ruth thought, disappearing into the kitchen. She could not have wished for a better neighbour surely. But why the move? And to a rented house? She had thought Francesca lived over the shop.

When she returned with the coffee, Francesca had quite settled herself in. 'I expect you are surprised to see me here,' she said, 'I – we've been living over the shop for several years.'

Ruth was not slow to hear the 'we' rather than 'I' and waited for her to go on.

'Martin, bless him is such a friend. You've met Martin, haven't you?'

'Yes.'

'Thank you.' She took the cup of coffee from Ruth. 'We grew up together – that happens in a village like Little Astons.'

'Yes,' Ruth said trying to keep the smile on her face natural.

'He's a poppet – always finds time to give a helping hand to a friend, even when—'

Ruth raised her eyebrows.

'No matter—'

'Sugar?' Ruth asked.

'No thanks, just as it is,' Francesca said.

She looked serious for a moment. 'Do you like it here?' she asked.

'Yes, very much,' Ruth said. 'I've settled in very well, considering.'

'Yes, I was told you had lost your husband recently.'

From Martin Amesbury? Ruth wondered. 'Almost a year ago,' Ruth said.

'I'm only here for a short time - I've taken the cottage on a six months' tenancy,' Francesca said.

It got more and more puzzling.

'I should explain,' Francesca went on. 'We are having a bungalow built, just outside Broughton, but it will not be ready for six months—'

'We?' Ruth asked.

'My husband, oh, I forgot, you didn't know I had a husband. Well, I am married to Alistair - Alistair Anderson. He has multiple sclerosis,' she said.

'Oh!' Ruth was shocked. 'I am sorry,' she began.

'Thank you. Well, there are problems, as you may imagine—'

'I can,' Ruth said, thinking how lucky she had been.

'He has had it for ten years,' she said. 'At first, well, you learn to live with it, but it is getting worse. He worked until five years ago. Now, I decided the time had come for me to give up the shop.'

'You're very brave,' Ruth said.

'It could be worse, couldn't it?' and Francesca smiled.

'We found a plot of land, and bought it, and decided when the time came we would build a bungalow so that Alistair won't be worried with stairs. We have planned it down to the last detail, but it won't be ready yet. So here I am, thanks to Martin.'

It passed through Ruth's mind - are they - were they - perhaps more than friends, then wondered what it had to do with her.

'Is your husband with you?'

'No, he's staying with his brother in Worcester until I'm

quite ready. But really nothing needs to be done now, Martin has seen to everything – it really is so comfortable. I must say I love the changes you have made. I remember it when the old man was alive. It was he who laid out the garden.'

'Yes, I thought perhaps it was.'

'You must come in and have a drink with us,' Francesca said. 'Alistair will enjoy that. And please call me Fran. You're Ruth, aren't you?'

Ruth smiled. 'You must let me know if there is anything I can do to help,' she said. 'Moving is quite an effort.'

'Yes, it is but everyone has been so helpful.'

'So you have sold the shop?'

'Yes, bit of a wrench, I've had it for fifteen years. Still, I'll be glad of the break, I've been at it too long and it's time I retired.'

Perhaps in her middle fifties, Ruth decided.

'Nice people have bought it though. Couple from London who wanted to retire to the Cotswolds. They're from Kensington.'

'Well, I hope they keep the shop as you used to,' Ruth said, 'although I haven't lived here long I always admired your window dressing.'

Francesca laughed. 'Oh, I enjoyed it. Still, everything comes to an end. When the bungalow gets really under way you must come and see it, it's not far – about four miles.'

'I know Broughton,' Ruth said. 'Pretty little village. My husband and I used to drive around the village all the time, looking forward to his retirement, but there – it was not to be. More coffee?'

'Please,' Francesca said. 'Have you children?'

'Yes, three – two boys and a girl – and four grandchildren.'

'We never had any,' Francesca said. 'In the beginning I never wanted them – the pull of the business was too much, then afterwards, when I decided I did, it was too late—'

'That must often happen,' Ruth said. She liked this

woman – she was easy to talk to – pity she wasn't staying. Still, she would make the most of it.

'Does your husband use a wheelchair?' she asked presently.

'Not all the time. It's useful if he wants to go out walking – he's not so good on his legs as he used to be. But we manage. We use the car a lot, and now I will have more time. He's going to love the cottage, I know,' and her face lit up at the thought. 'He hasn't seen it since we first decided to take it. Now that it's been done over, he will be delighted. I can't wait for him to see it.'

'When is he coming?' Ruth asked, feeling quite excited herself.

'His brother is bringing him home on Sunday,' Francesca said.

'Look – are you doing anything – lunch time?' Ruth asked.

Francesca would be busy once her husband came home. 'Why don't we go out to lunch?' she said. 'To celebrate. My treat.'

'Oh!' Francesca looked quite shocked at the suggestion. Then she gave a big smile.

'That would be lovely!' she said, and glanced at her watch.

'Just locally,' Ruth said. 'See you around twelve-thirty?'

Two days later she decided to call on Miss Willis. It was time she paid her another visit.

She bought a small bunch of colourful asters not wishing to overdo the gifts and knowing they would last. The girl, Rose, this time allowed her in without query.

'I've come to see Miss Willis,' Ruth smiled.

'Yes, go on up – you know where she is.'

Ruth tapped on the door.

Miss Willis came to answer it and her usually austere face widened into a smile.

Really, Ruth thought, she is quite attractive.

'Ruth, how nice of you to come - come in - are those for me?'

She took the flowers. 'Oh, my father used to grow asters - loved them—'

'Yes, they're such a lovely colour.'

'Do sit down. It is so nice to see you. You quite make my day . . .'

Ruth looked around. Really it was quite a pleasant room and adequate for Miss Willis's personal needs.

'Well, Edith, have you been out or doing anything nice?'

Edith put a kettle on. 'As a matter of fact, I have. I walked down to the library van. Janet told me where to find it, and it stops outside the village hall - a nice young man driver, and a library lady - very knowledgeable - so we talked of books and she was very helpful.'

She would have enjoyed that, thought Ruth.

As Miss Willis made the coffee, Ruth made up her mind. 'I've been thinking,' she said. 'I know you have good food in here, but I wondered - would you care to join me for lunch one day in the village?'

Miss Willis beamed at her. 'I should love it!' she said. 'Something to look forward to - do you get lonely sometimes, Ruth? Losing your husband suddenly like that?'

'I do,' sighed Ruth. 'I think all women who are left do. It's only natural. You miss the companionship - it takes a time to learn to live on your own. Of course, you have people here.'

'Well, that was why I came but they are not always the sort of person you would choose to be with,' Edith said. 'Mrs Bancroft is very nice, but she is not awfully well at the moment and Mrs Bligh - well, the less said about her the better,' and her face resumed its natural grim expression.

She handed Ruth a cup of coffee. 'No sugar, isn't it - I remember that from the teacher's staff room,' and they both laughed.

'Well, it's not all that long ago,' conceded Ruth. 'Now,

how about next Tuesday – I'll pick you up at twelve-thirty, is that all right?'

Miss Willis beamed. 'I shall look forward to it.'

Chapter Twelve

It was Miss Willis's birthday. She was seventy.

She had dreaded this day arriving – but she felt no different. She took her early morning cup of tea back to bed with her and lay for a long time reflecting on the past.

The year she had been at Greystones had been awful. There were times when she hadn't wanted to go on – thought she couldn't go on. Twenty-five years their relationship had lasted, hers and Charmian's – even her name was delightful. Small and rounded, with such laughing blue eyes, rosy cheeks – she was everything a girl should be. Not like her, tall, angular, bony Edith.

As a teacher she had been disliked, positively feared by those girls but once Charmian had joined them, her life had taken on another perspective. Charmian was drawn to her too, she didn't see Miss Willis the way everyone else did. She saw her as tall and brave and someone to be relied on.

And that dear little house – full of all their treasures – how could she have stayed on there after Charmian died? Why did she die? She was only ill two days – had never been ill – she couldn't believe it. Sixty-three – what an age to die – and surrounded by the lovely things they had brought back from holidays in the Tyrol, the Black Forest, Czechoslovakia, except that it wasn't called that now, Switzerland – she had kept the cow bells, they were in a drawer. Every time she picked them up and they tinkled their nostalgic bells, she thought of Charmian.

Those pretty little dresses she wore – she never ever wore trousers or skirts, unless the skirts were frilly, or great woolly jumpers or cardigans. She wore blouses, and scarves, and pretty high-heeled shoes.

She put her cup down. Well, now was the beginning of the rest of her life, and if she went on living as she had been this past year, it would be hell.

Now that Ruth Durling had come along, it made a difference. Someone who knew her, called her Edith – brought her flowers – and now she was going out to lunch.

She must make a resolution – to live the rest of her life, whatever there was of it without reference to Charmian. She was on her own, like so many people. She had courage, she had had to have, being a dour sort of girl brought up in Scotland, although she was only part Scottish.

She thought of her parents, working out their lives in that harsh Highland country, how they had skimped and saved to give her a decent education – and jumped out of bed to her feet.

I could, she thought, with her first optimistic thought of the day, be crippled with arthritis ... But Janet comes today ...

Following her usual pattern, and carrying library books for the old lady on the top floor, Janet took off her boots once inside Greystones on this wet November morning and changed into her flat shoes. It was warm outside, although the rain was falling steadily, and after depositing her books and having a word with the elderly patient, she went downstairs to see Miss Willis first.

She tapped on the door, and Miss Willis called out, 'Come in!' not something she usually did, then greeted Janet with, 'Good morning, Janet, a wet one,' and went herself to get the towel to put round her shoulders.

'Good morning, Miss Willis – just a shampoo today?'

'Please, I want it to look nice for Tuesday.'

'Going somewhere nice?'

'Yes, I'm going to lunch at Gennaro's with Ruth, Mrs Durling.'

'Oh, that will be lovely,' Janet said, and she was pleased. How good it was of Ruth to bother with her - she had always been so difficult - but Ruth obviously understood her.

Rubbing the conditioner into Miss Willis's thin hair, her mind was on Mrs Bancroft who had not been at all well when last she called.

Rinsing off the conditioner, she towelled the hair dry, then began to blow dry it.

'We have a new person coming in on this floor,' Miss Willis said, proferring information that was not her usual way. 'You remember Mrs Lanscombe who died, well, this woman is taking her place. A widow, I believe.'

'Oh,' Janet said, only slightly recalling Mrs Lanscombe, who had chosen to go each week to Luigi's where she said she had been a client for years.

'No spray?' she asked.

Miss Willis shuddered. 'No thank you,' she said. 'Very nice, dear.'

Praise indeed, thought Janet, taking her leave, and going along to see Mrs Bancroft, tapping gently on the door.

'Come in,' said the low soft voice, and Janet found her client still in bed.

'Hello, there, having a rest day, are we?'

Mrs Bancroft gave a weak smile. 'I thought I wouldn't get up until lunch time today.'

'Why should you?' Janet said staunchly. 'If you feel like a lie in, you should. What did the doctor say on Friday?'

She took one of Mrs Bancroft's hands in her own firm grip. How thin and frail it still was - there was no life in it.

'He wants me to go for a scan or something. My heart is behaving erratically, something about a bypass maybe but I wouldn't—'

'What do you mean – you wouldn't – the treatment these days is wonderful.'

'I'm only scared Mrs Woolsbridge will ask me to leave,' Mrs Bancroft said. 'I mean, I'm settled here. I've been here four years, and you know how she won't keep anyone if they are really ill.'

'Oh, you're not really ill – just having a bit of a blip,' Janet smiled reassuringly. 'Are you eating?' she went on.

'Not really – I'm not hungry.'

'Oh, you'll feel better when you get over this,' Janet said. 'So no hair today?'

'I really should—'

'Look, we'll make it next week – it won't hurt to leave it while you are feeling under the weather.'

'Tell me how you are, Janet. I don't hear any news in here.'

'Well, my son Ralph is coming home again this weekend – not with that girl he has, she is at Cambridge.'

'She must be clever, Janet,' Mrs Bancroft said wistfully.

'Yes, I think she is.' No need to tell her she had seen Luigi last week and discussed the situation of his giving up the salon next year. He would want her to have it, she knew, but it was the money and it would curtail her visits to the nursing home. Anyway, it was a long way off yet.

'More new neighbours in Notcutts Lane,' she said. 'Renting.'

'Renting? Oh that's a change.'

'Yes, apparently Mr Amesbury has bought the house and is going to rent it out – the antiques man, you know.'

'Oh, I do indeed. Such a charming man. I've bought many things in that lovely shop. Pity about the wife, though.'

'Yes,' Janet said, 'but he's better off without her.'

Mrs Bancroft began to look quite animated. 'Still, he'll miss her – in the shop, I mean.'

'Well, anyway, it's been let to Francesca, Francesca Anderson, who has the dress shop.'

'Oh, yes, I know her. Very nice things. Is she closing down?'

'Yes, she has sold the dress shop and will be moving to Broughton in six months' time.'

'Oh, I'm sorry to hear that.'

'She has a husband with multiple sclerosis.'

'Oh, how dreadful!'

'So they are building a bungalow which will be ready in six months, hopefully, for them.'

Mrs Bancroft sighed heavily. 'Oh, some people are dreadfully unlucky, aren't they? Such trouble and she is only young.'

'Yes, he's no more than fifty-five.'

'Well, I must say, that really does make you count your blessings,' Mrs Bancroft said.

Janet could see that she had made her feel quite sad and was sorry now that she had told her.

'Well, what can I get you – bring you in – sweeties, fruit? Has your daughter been in?'

'No but she is coming in on Sunday.'

'Good,' Janet said firmly. 'Well, I must go – see you next week. Don't you worry about the Andersons – they are moving into a really lovely little home and he is improving all the time – they've got some wonderful new treatments for MS.' Fingers crossed, she thought.

Outside, she gave a deep sigh. Mrs Bancroft didn't look at all well.

It would be a different story in Mrs Bligh's room. And it was.

'"I'll be your sweetheart – if you will be mine,"' came through the door as Janet approached – not a song she knew, but she guessed it would be an old-time song, and there was no doubting Mrs Bligh's strong voice.

She tapped on the door. 'Hello there and how are we today?'

'Oh, my dear,' and Mrs Bligh gave a loud laugh. 'Just fine, my dear. On top of the world.'

'Well, that's great,' Janet said. 'What to do today then?'
'Oh, the usual.'
'And I don't think I can colour today, I've got rather a rush on – I have to go to the tailor's to see about a new suit for my eldest boy.'
'Oh, my dear, you go when you've finished. Just the usual shampoo. I think the colour has held quite well, don't you?'
'It's great,' Janet said.
The face with its closed eyes below her, had an upturned mouth, almost a smile. Life was good, Janet thought, for Mrs Bligh. With her trips out and her old friends, she was one of the lucky ones.
She rinsed the red hair, darker now because it was wet, and towelled it dry, then began to blow dry.
'You're quiet today,' Mrs Bligh said.
'Who? Me? Sorry,' Janet said. 'I'm thinking about lots of things all at once.'
'Nothing worrying, dear?' Mrs Bligh said. She sounded concerned, for she was basically a kind woman. 'What sort of suit will you have in mind?'
'Well, I'll see what Brooks have. I don't want to leave him on his own to buy it – you never know what they'll choose, so I'll look around first. It will be his first new suit and he's going to need it for all sorts of things, interviews, that sort of thing. There, how is that?' Janet asked.
Mrs Bligh patted here and there. 'Yes, that's fine, dear. I'll just put my earrings back in – that's it.'
'Well, I'll see you next week,' Janet said. 'Have fun.'
'That's likely in here.' Mrs Bligh made a face.
Janet walked along the High Street, passing Luigi's again, and thinking how much she would like to have that little shop. She knew she could make a go of it, but chance would be a fine thing.
She turned into Crisp Street and there was Eden Brook, as usual, serving a customer in his tailor's shop.
She waited, looking around, until he was free, when he

looked up and smiled. His face was so familiar to her, she had known him since she was sixteen and he eighteen. It was a manly face now, sharpened by the years; gone were the round cheeks of adolescence, the boyish look of innocence; instead there were lines finely etched on his cheeks, and a furrow between his brows, still dark, and now smiling.

'Janet,' he said, putting a box back on the shelf. 'Socks all right?'

'Yes, fine, thanks, Eden. But I'm here because I think Ralph needs a suit – you know a nice one and before I send him in, I thought I'd look around and see what you have.'

'You don't need me to tell you that they mostly want jeans, T-shirts—'

'Eden, I know, but I would like him to have a proper suit – there must be times at college when he needs to be decently dressed. Can you show me some swatches of material?'

'Surely.' He went to a shelf and brought out several thick little sample books, thumbing them back. 'This one makes up well – I've just made it up for a young City man. I haven't seen Ralph for ages – what size is he?'

'I don't know exactly, it's ages since I bought anything for him that needed fitting. It's usually jeans and jerseys and fleeces or whatever they call them.' She smiled. 'Well, I like what I've seen – you've got a good selection – I hope he will. I'll send him in, probably Saturday, if I can get him to move.'

'Not easy, is it, Jan?' he asked.

She was taken by surprise, and stared at him.

'Bringing up two lads—'

'Oh, they're good boys and I still seem to have some influence on them, thank goodness.'

Seeing how friendly he was, she thought she might mention to him taking over Luigi's, since he was in the local Chamber of Commerce, and it was no secret that she wanted the shop.

'I tell you what,' she said slowly. 'When you have time,

Eden, I would like a word with you – about business.'

He frowned. 'Business?'

'Luigi.' She mouthed the word in case anyone was listening. 'I'd like your advice.'

'Oh, yes. See what you mean, well . . .'

She hoped she had not been too forward mentioning it – anyway it was done now and she waited.

'Well,' he said slowly. 'How about coming out for a meal one evening, at say, the Besford Arms? Next Tuesday or Wednesday?'

Why had he chosen to go just outside the village? she wondered. The Besford Arms was a small hotel, and smart. She hadn't expected that.

'No?' he queried.

'If you're sure,' she said, and suddenly smiled. 'I'd like that,' she added and, so unused was she to being asked out, 'Let's go Dutch, shall we?'

'No, Jan,' he said firmly. 'My treat. I'll pick you up on Tuesday around seven – will that be all right?'

'Yes, yes, that's fine.'

'See you then . . .'

She was going out. She had a date. She was being picked up by car and taken to dinner. She felt as though she was walking on air. And Eden Brook, too . . .

After Janet had gone, Mrs Bligh sat staring at herself in the mirror. Nell, she told herself. You look awful . . . Old, lined, she peered more closely at herself . . . No good hiding from the truth. And that swine not turning up, well, she might have known. He had his free lunch and that was that . . . but you had to keep up appearances – like Hyacinth. Now that was a name which would have suited her. Instead of Ellen, called Nell. Still, everyone knew her as Nell – all the regulars that is . . .

It was like the stage, really. You were an actress. No matter what – you had to go downstairs to open the bar, and put on a cheerful smile. All those years. 'Hi, Nell, how're doin', Nell, have one on me, Nell,' no matter how you were feeling.

You might have known that your husband had not come to bed until three, you might have known he was sleeping with the new barmaid – hussy – but you still had to get up and pretend everything was all right.

Your best dress or outfit, made up to the nines – nails perfectly manicured, hair done, perfume, earrings, the low-cut blouses just enough to promise what was underneath but no more, to tickle their fancies – men!

And you couldn't easily give up what you'd done for a lifetime – make up, dressing up, the naughty twinkle in your eye, promising what you seldom gave, the big smile, the sympathetic ear – men!

She felt a bit like Ethel Merman in that old song – there's no business like show business – true – she'd long forgotten what her true self was like, and now she didn't much care.

She flexed her aching knees and stood up. She wasn't going anywhere but she felt like dressing up a bit. The navy satin skirt – cost an arm and a leg – the scarlet fichu-like blouse, the ruby earrings . . .

She tried to twirl her knee – she had been good at that in the old days – she had started out in the chorus at the Palladium – but fell back on to her chair. She laughed out loud. Well, you had to laugh – all life was a joke.

Then she sobered up and went over to the wardrobe, singing 'I will survive . . .' It was her favourite song.

Chapter Thirteen

On opposite sides of the Lamb car park there were two cars. The Lamb was quite a way from Little Astons, as it needed to be, for the two car owners went out of their way to choose the spot of their assignation carefully. Sometimes it was in town, sometimes at some distance, as this was, some forty miles away in a little village in an obscure corner of the Chilterns.

They saw each other infrequently now, over the years the meetings had become rarer. Having once seen the beautiful Lady Bankes, she was not easily forgotten, and could have been recognised. On these occasions, though, she wore jeans and sunglasses, her glorious hair tied back, an old raincoat, which had seen better days, unless they were meeting in town, which usually meant that her husband was abroad.

The need to see each other, if only occasionally, had always been with them but they had not met since the day that Ruth had spotted them in London.

Now, they were inside the Lamb, in a cosy dark corner. The Lamb was a real old country pub and they were having a makeshift lunch. But they looked troubled, both of them, and there was no holding of hands across the table.

Fenella toyed with her red wine, her eyes not on Eden but on the glass she was playing with. They had obviously said what they had to say to each other and were mulling it over.

Finally, Eden broke the silence. 'It is pointless, Fen,' he said. 'It's time you got on with your life and I with mine.'

'You've met someone else,' she said.

'I meet many women,' he said, 'but that's not to say I am serious about them.'

'Then why—'

'Because I've got to the stage when I find it - disturbing,' he said. 'You're always there, in the background, no matter what I do. I feel - sort of tied to you.'

'You are,' she said.

'I'm not,' Eden said firmly. 'What we had was a long time ago - years ago.'

'So why can't we stay friends?'

'Oh come on, Fen!' For the first time he showed a flicker of irritation. 'You've got a super husband—'

'You didn't think so when I married him. You said you could have killed him—'

'Yes, I did feel that,' he acknowledged. 'But - we're older. I know after all these years you are not for me - and face it, Fen - you are happy with him, aren't you?'

She finally looked up, her speedwell-blue eyes looking into his dark ones, which almost floored him. 'I know I'm spoiled, Eden,' she said. 'I love you both.'

He regarded her. 'I need to get on with my life.'

She looked at him suspiciously. 'You *have* met someone else.'

'No, but I'm thinking I don't want to go on like this for the rest of my life. I'm in my forties, Fen. And I would have liked a family.'

'Oh, don't!' she cried out, her hand covering her face.

'Is that unreasonable?' he asked her, seemingly unmoved this time by her agitation.

'No, no, no, of course not,' and she put out a hand to cover his, but he removed it. He knew he had to be firm. He must be firm. Otherwise this would go on for ever and these hole-in-the-corner meetings - rare though they now were - were becoming unbearable.

'So you mean – we're never to see each other again,' she said.

'That's being a bit dramatic,' he said. 'I'm trying to be practical. Let's make this the last time we meet like this – in this surreptitious way. After all, we've done nothing to be ashamed of. We can stay friends.'

'And when are we likely to see each other?' she asked him, her beautiful mouth downturned, her wide eyes beseeching his.

He had known it was going to be difficult. They had never even attempted before to bring an end to their meetings. But he knew he was right. Lately, he had found himself becoming impatient with himself. Irritated, wondering what he was playing at.

'Let's have coffee,' he said.

When the waiter brought the coffee, they both drank it black.

'And how is little Margot?'

Margot was her youngest child, her seven-year-old daughter. 'Better thanks. She had a bad dose of flu but antibiotics, you know . . .'

She sat staring into her coffee cup, and then she looked up, blue eyes wide, nostrils dilating. 'Eden, I'm pregnant!'

He sat back in total shock. It was the last thing he had expected her to say. He knew it wasn't his. That side of their relationship had fizzled out years ago.

'Christ,' he said, then took a deep breath and sat back, and smiled.

'What a super note to end it on,' he said, and raised his wine glass. 'Here's to you both,' he said.

He called the waiter over for the bill and gave him his card. Nothing was said, then the waiter returned with his card. She kept her head lowered. He couldn't tell whether or not she was crying. 'I'll see you to your car,' he said eventually and escorted her out of the Lamb and towards the waiting car.

'Good luck, Fen,' he said. 'Good luck to you and your

family. 'Stay well.' And he was gone.

That afternoon, Ruth had a call from Julie, and she had the feeling that she was calling from the Park Lane flat.

'Oh, lovely to hear your voice!' Julie said. 'Is everything all right?'

'Yes, how about you?'

'I'm fine – we have just got back from Dorchester where we spent the weekend.'

'Oh, that made a change!'

'Yes, Douglas King is a friend of Bertie's, and his wife is very nice. She made us very welcome and Bertie was as well as I have ever seen him.'

'Oh, that's good, then.'

'What I rang about, Ruth dear, was wondering if you could come up to town one day next week?'

'Love to,' said Ruth. 'Any special day?'

'Well, Wednesday would be good – come to lunch – we'll go to my dear little flat and have a drink and a sandwich.'

'That would be lovely,' Ruth said, and she meant it. It would only mean a telephone call to Dolly to tell her she would not be at the Red Cross gathering that afternoon.

'Come about eleven – I've lots to tell you.'

Oh, that was nice ... She liked surprises, something to look forward to.

On Tuesday evening, Janet was making a special effort to look her best.

She had only been to the Besford Arms once or twice back in the old days, and knew it to be rather expensive. Bearing that in mind, she made up carefully, and wore a little black dress, her one expensive item she had bought in Spain but, being well cut and from a designer sale, she knew she looked her best. (She wore a rope of pearls and small pearl earrings, and brushed her hair until it shone.)

David was playing football, and would be in later, so she

had left his meal in the fridge with instructions to microwave. She often wondered as a working woman how she would have managed without this instant oven.

She was ready early, far too early, and sat doing her nails and glancing out of the window for Eden's car, for although the Besford Arms was less than a mile out of town, she knew they would go by car.

Presently, her heart beating uncomfortably, she saw his car coming down the narrow drive. He stopped, and came to the door. She hoped he didn't see the fluttering in her throat when she opened the door to him, and stood aside for him to enter.

He observed the pleasantly furnished little cottage with its shining brass and copper, the table in the hall with its bowl of flowers.

'This looks good, Jan,' he said. 'I haven't been in one of these cottages before.'

'Really, well, come in for a moment. Would you like a drink before we go? I have some wine.'

'No, thanks,' he said. 'We'll have one when we get there.' He walked through to the doors leading to the garden. 'I say, it's very pretty out there. You back on to the old orchard, don't you?'

'Yes – that's why they called all these cottages the Fruit Cottages and left us some fruit trees in the garden – which is handy.'

'I envy you,' he said. 'I only have a yard.'

She wanted to say – you can come and sit in my garden any time you like. He was still as fanciable as he had ever been. Older, but if anything better looking. There was an air of stability about him. He could never be as good looking as Jack but see where that had got her. Anyway, what was she thinking? She had merely been asked out to dinner.

He turned. 'Where's David?' he asked.

'Football,' and she made a face. 'Where else. I wish he would give half his enthusiasm for football to his lessons.'

'Oh, come on, Janet. You can't complain. Young Ralph did very well.'

'Yes, I'm very proud of him.' She picked up her handbag from the table, and he took the hint.

'Well, let's go, shall we?'

The drive was short, and he parked in the hotel car park, coming round to the passenger door to open it for her.

'Thanks.' Oh, it was nice to be taken out, escorted for the evening – her life had been very short on this kind of thing since she'd got back from Spain. She was going to make the most of this.

Once inside, they were led to a corner seat, a table for two, with discreet table lamps, but not too dark to see the menu or the wine list which the waiter handed to Eden.

'Would you like a pre-dinner drink, or settle for wine, that is, we could have gone to the bar.'

She shook her head. 'Oh, no, thank you, I'd like wine.'

'Do you have a preference – red, white?'

'I think white, because I fancy fish, if it's on the menu.'

He looked pleased. He obviously appreciated a woman who knew her own mind. Having sorted the wine with the waiter, he picked up the menu, and offered her another one – without the prices.

Oh, very pleasing, Janet thought. Having settled for a simple starter, Janet chose a sole, and Eden did the same.

The wine waiter arrived and poured the wine, which Eden declared very good, and Janet wondered if he did this often. Perhaps he took many women out – she would have no idea.

Well, she thought, this is my night and I am loving every minute of it.

They talked briefly of this and that, village news, what was going on in the immediate neighbourhood. He asked Janet if she knew Martin's wife had left him.

'I thought everyone knew that,' laughed Janet. 'Poor old Martin – it was a bit of a blow.'

'Not so old,' Eden said. 'In his sixties, I should imagine,

but she was his business partner, which makes it worse.'

They had finished their sole, and sat back before ordering a dessert. He looked across at her.

'Well, Jan,' he said. 'We should have done this before.' She found herself blushing, and lowered her eyes.

'No one more surprised than me, when the news came of your divorce. I would have thought of all the couples I know yours was the soundest marriage.'

'Which just goes to prove – something or other,' Janet smiled.

'Anyway, tell me about your plans to take over Luigi's premises.'

'Rather, I would say, that's what I would *like* to do – whether or not it is possible, is the question.'

'What would hold you up?' he asked.

'Well, a good offer that I couldn't match from someone else.'

'I haven't heard that anyone else is after it but then I wouldn't know all the answers,' Eden said. 'I only know that his lease is up next June and he is not going to renew it.'

'Well, that's something,' Janet said. She could hardly tell him that the price would hold her back. She had even thought of leaving the cottage and moving to the rooms over the shop, but it wouldn't be fair on the boys. In any case, she loved Plum Tree Cottage; she had bought it as a refuge when she came back from Spain and she intended to hold on to it if she could.

'Anyway, he does well there, doesn't he?' she asked.

'I should say – he's only giving up because he is too old and his two sons prefer to live in Italy, so no one in the family wants to take over.'

'Oh,' Janet said. 'I think I have a chance.' Who knew what would happen between now and next June?

'And how are you, Eden?' she said, daring to ask.

'Me? I'm fine,' he said.

'I thought I'd come back from Spain to find you married

and settled down.' He had the grace to look uncomfortable. Couldn't look at her.

'You're not still – oh, Eden!'

His face was grim. 'We've finished,' he said.

'I should think so,' she said with a grin trying to lighten the situation. 'She's been married – what – about sixteen years – must be and has two children.' But she knew from the look on his face that it really wasn't over. He must be mad. What chance did he have? Suddenly she thought, suppose, suppose, they really were in love with each other, and that wretched mother of hers – oh, surely not?

He looked like a man wrestling with his conscience, when the waiter interrupted with the dessert trolley. A dessert was the last thing on Janet's mind, but she asked for *crème-brûlée* and Eden ordered cheese.

By the time the coffee came, the atmosphere had stabilised somewhat. She had had time to digest what he had told her and inwardly was furious – with her ladyship, so called, who kept him dangling on a string – or was it him who pestered her?

What hope was there for the pair of them? How could she? Eden should be happily married by now, with children of his own, but perhaps he was the sort of man to indulge in a clandestine affair. It wasn't for her to suggest that he marry and settle down. That would be too obvious.

For seeing him again at close quarters – she realised, again, how attractive he was. He would be to most women. What a waste!

She could think of nothing nicer than sharing a home with Eden but that wasn't to be. Always hankering after another woman, someone he couldn't have – how stupid. And Janet was the sort of woman who would lose patience very easily. Particularly when something was hopeless or out of the question.

Fenella indeed. Keeping him on a string, dangling like some monkey. She wanted it all. Her anger gave her the audacity to ask what she did.

'Do you still see her?'

He looked shocked. But he was honest. She knew he wouldn't lie.

'Sometimes, but, well, it is over now.'

After all these years? She couldn't help the puzzled, questioning look which she knew had come to her face.

She put a hand over his. 'I'm sorry, Eden. It is none of my business. I am just sorry that—' She couldn't say 'wasted your life' – perhaps he hadn't. He seemed perfectly happy.

She attacked her *crème-brûlée* half heartedly. 'Lovely meal,' she said, putting down her spoon.

He looked at her, his fine eyes so open and honest that she felt like crying. For a waste of his youth, for that blasted Fenella, who through her beauty had ensnared a young man . . .

Oh, come on, she told herself, you're not a romantic novelist. She took a deep breath. 'I really did enjoy that, Eden,' she said, coming down to earth with a bang.

'So did I,' he said. 'We must do it again sometime. I'm sorry I wasn't much help about the shop but you will have to see how events pan out.'

'Well, as long as you think I would be doing the right thing.'

'I can't be sure of that – it depends how much it is going to cost you. Will it affect the boys – your running a business?'

'I don't think so. Ralph is off my hands almost and young David is almost thirteen and before you know it he will be away at college too, I hope. I expect he wants to fall into Beckham's shoes but that's not likely. No, they will be all right. I would never let them suffer, but I am sure I could make a go of it.'

He smiled at her. 'I am sure you could.'

In silence they drove the short way home.

When he stopped the car, and allowed her to get out, she looked up at him. 'Thank you, Eden,' she said, her brown eyes frank and warm.

He bent and lightly kissed her. 'Goodnight, Jan.'

He reversed up the drive, and unlocking the front door, she saw a light under the kitchen door.

'All right, David?'

He grinned back at her. 'All right, Mum. Have a good time?'

'Yes, thank you, David,' she said, thinking that was the understatement of the year.

Chapter Fourteen

Although it was November, it was a mild, windless day but, with leaves scattered everywhere, there could be no doubt in anyone's mind that autumn had arrived.

Ruth closed the front door behind her, and unlocking the car, stepped inside and drove herself to the station.

She was always pleased to be going up to town, especially when it involved seeing Julie. It would be the first time she would visit her as a married woman and she was interested to see if married life had changed her.

There was the usual queue at Paddington, but she managed to get a taxi fairly soon, and in no time was in Orchard Street. She stopped off to buy a huge sheaf of roses in Selfridges and once inside the block of flats, the porter smiled at her.

He knew her of old, there was no need to give her name as she got into the lift; although they were much more fussy now about visitors than they had been years ago.

'Nice day, madam,' he said.

'Yes, very pleasant,' she answered, and pressed the bell for the second floor.

Walking along to Julie's flat, she noticed that the hall had been redecorated, and a surprising number of people were about.

She pressed the bell, and Julie came at once. 'Oh, Ruth, how lovely, thank you.' She took the roses and put them on the hall table, throwing her arms around Ruth and they hugged each other.

'Come in, nothing has changed.' Julie smiled. Inside it was indeed as charming as ever, full of colour, and lovely things to look at. In the small sitting room, the coffee table had been laid – there were biscuits and a pot of coffee.

'Just let me put these in water. I timed it well, I know when I say eleven, you'll be here on time.'

'Well, I always knew time was important to you and, as a teacher, it was important to me too. Have you noticed how things have changed? When people say ten or two, they are frequently at least half an hour late.'

'Yes, I can't bear it,' Julie said, 'I could never have run my business on those terms, but the traffic is so bad in London now that sometimes it just can't be helped.'

They were both playing with words and presently Ruth sat down and began to relax. It was a different set-up, somehow, not like the old days, and remembering, she took Julie's left hand.

'Let me see,' she said, and, on Julie's finger saw the platinum wedding ring, and above it, a magnificent diamond, a solitaire – goodness knows how many carats it must have been.

'Oh, Julie,' she breathed, 'it is beautiful.' Julie smiled, looking down at it. 'Yes, it is rather. Excuse me, let me get the coffee.'

She was different, or was Ruth imagining it? She decided to be practical. 'Well, how is it working out? You're living, of course, in Park Lane.'

'Yes, but I pop back here sometimes,' Julie said.

'And how is Bertie?'

'Very well. He uses the wheelchair more, of course, because his gout is playing him up but really, it is no problem – we go into the park sometimes, he likes that.'

'Do you take him?' Ruth asked.

'Well, of course. He likes me to do it. There is Norah,

of course, and a nurse comes in sometimes, but he likes me to be there – more coffee?'

'Thanks,' Ruth said.

'And how is life in Little Astons?'

'Interesting. I feel I've been there for years,' and Ruth proceeded to tell her about her activities, Miss Willis, and the new neighbours next door.

'Watch out, Ruth,' Julie said. 'Don't make a rod for your own back.'

Which was surprising advice, Ruth thought, seeing whence it came. 'Oh, at the moment I am enjoying it,' she said and talked of Janet and somehow didn't mention Martin Amesbury, who was often uppermost in her mind.

She finished her coffee. 'Now, how is life with you, Julie? Pleased at what you have done – the decision you made?'

Julie put down her coffee cup and Ruth noticed that her hand was shaking a little. Her eyes were extraordinarily bright, those lovely dark eyes which were her best feature, shining as though with unshed tears.

'Yes, of course,' she said. 'Life is different but Bertie is very good to me – I can have whatever I want – you would be surprised what the Park Lane flat looks like now. It was wonderful to shop around with money no object – it adds a different flavour to shopping I can tell you.'

'I imagine,' Ruth said, never having experienced it herself. Was money that important to Julie? Had that been the reason she married Bertie Stringer? She had never thought so but you never, however long you lived, really know another person . . .

Julie cleared away the coffee things; it was by now around midday. 'I'll get us a nice gin and tonic – I've already made the sandwiches.'

'What is Bertie doing for lunch today?' Ruth asked.

'Oh, Norah will see to him. I have to have some time to myself, I told him. Remember I was a working girl until I married him but he doesn't like to be reminded of that.'

Ruth thought there was an unlived-in feeling about the flat – or did she imagine that too? It could never be the same now, without the clients and Julie bustling about in her white coat, and she had a moment's regret for what used to be.

Julie reappeared with a tray on which stood two sparkling glasses of gin and tonic with ice and lemon.

'Here's to us,' she said, handing one to Ruth.

'To you and Bertie. Remember, I haven't toasted your health yet. Here's to you both.'

'Thank you, it's lovely to see old friends.'

Ruth put down her glass. 'How did the wedding go?'

'Very well – it was quiet – that was the way we wanted it and afterwards we had a slap-up lunch at the Ritz.'

'Lovely,' said Ruth.

'Let me get the sandwiches,' Julie said, 'they're all ready.'

Ruth sipped her gin and tonic, noticing that Julie's had almost disappeared. Returning with the neatly made smoked salmon sandwiches, she went back into the kitchen and came back with a refilled glass.

'So, you've quite settled in at Apple Tree Cottage,' she said. 'That didn't take you long.'

'Well, I moved in May, so that's about seven months but it's easier to settle in a small village – you quickly get to know people.'

'I suppose,' Julie said. 'Help yourself.'

By the time they had finished the sandwiches, Ruth had drunk her gin and tonic.

'Another?' Julie asked. 'Go on, be a devil.'

'No, really, I can't – that was a large one and I want to go round the shops this afternoon. I shall be too tight to see anything.'

'Oh, well, I'm going to.' And Julie disappeared into the kitchen to return with another full glass, and by now, she was definitely not her usual urbane self; her steady stare from her level brown eyes was not in evidence and she evidently found it difficult to focus.

I wonder, thought Ruth, how much she had had before I arrived. Was that what I smelled on her breath? She was not used to the smell of gin, she was a wine drinker, while John had liked his glass of whisky.

She suddenly felt a sense of unease but told herself not to be such a misery. Julie seemed to be happy enough. It was she, Ruth, who was making a mountain out of a molehill. Nevertheless, she decided to make a move.

'Well, that was lovely,' she said. 'A super lunch. Shall I take these things into the kitchen?'

'Thanks,' Julie said. 'I suppose I'd better get back too, or his lordship will be—' But she didn't finish the sentence.

Ruth picked up her handbag. 'Now when shall I see you again? I suppose there is no chance of your coming down to see me?'

And Julie looked shocked. 'Oh, no dear! No chance! Still, you must come up to town again.' But she made no effort to detain Ruth as she walked to the front door.

They kissed. 'Thank you for a lovely lunch.'

'Take care,' Julie said. 'Give me a ring.'

'I will.' With a wave, Ruth made her way along the corridor to the lift with a feeling of sadness that she couldn't shift.

The next day, Ruth called at Greystones to pick up Miss Willis for lunch.

She was already waiting in the hall when Ruth arrived, dressed in a camel coat, belted, and a rather outdated felt hat, which somehow suited her. No hair showed beneath the hat, which gave her a mannish appearance, but she looked quite smartly noticeable.

'I thought we'd walk – it's only up the road,' Ruth said. 'Do you have any mobility problems – so many people do?'

'No, thank goodness,' Edith Willis said. 'These skinny legs of mine are like a pair of walking sticks.'

She was in a good mood, probably happy at the thought

of being taken out to lunch and Ruth was pleased she had suggested it.

Gennaro's was warm and inviting inside and they took a table for two.

The menu was mainly Italian, although they served other food. 'What do you think?' Ruth asked. 'I hope you like Italian food.'

'Love it,' Edith Willis said firmly. 'One of the reasons Charmian and I went abroad so much was to sample the food, especially French and Italian. This seems to be quite comprehensive.' She devoured the menu with avid eyes.

'One of my favourite meals was Italian Stuffed Aubergines. I simply love aubergines and we don't get those often at Greystones.'

'They have them here,' Ruth said. 'I think I'll have that – I don't bother half as much with food now that I am on my own.'

'Well, Charmian was the cook – and a good one.'

So she missed her in more ways than one. 'That's what I'm going to have. Shall we have a starter?'

'No, not for me if I'm having aubergines and then maybe I'll get around to a pudding, not my usual indulgence.'

'What about a glass of wine?' Ruth asked. 'A glass of house red?'

'Great,' she said, as they ordered and sat back to await their meal.

'By the way, Ruth, I was going to ask you – are you still a member of the Fine Arts?'

'No, I never was, you mean the Cheltenham branch?'

'Yes, oh, well, perhaps you won't be interested.'

'I am in anything these days with possibilities. Antiques isn't it? I was never bothered enough to go to meetings – always too interested in the garden.'

'Antiques and lectures, that sort of thing – trips out sometimes – once a month it used to be. No, why I ask, is that I still get the usual notice of meetings, and Rokebys are coming to little Astons – can you believe it – next month, the beginning of December.'

'The antiques people – from London?'

'Yes, you know, along the lines of the *Antiques Road Show* on television.'

'Oh, I always watch that,' Ruth said.

'Well, it is for charity – the Heart Foundation – and you take along whatever you want – within reason and they value it. Tickets a fiver. I thought it would be quite interesting. Well, I am going anyway – it will be something to do. It's on a Tuesday evening sometime in December. I have one or two things we collected I would like valued.'

'I would like that,' Ruth exclaimed.

'Apparently, a local man is chairing it and judging china. He is an expert on oriental china and porcelain – isn't that interesting?'

'Oh, who is that?' Ruth asked.

'A man called Martin Amesbury. Apparently he has a shop in the High Street.'

And for some unaccountable reason Ruth's heart began to beat faster. That, she thought, she would like to see.

'Well, I shall definitely be coming to that,' she said firmly. 'Are you getting the tickets, Edith, or are they at the door?'

'I think we just turn up. They have no idea how many people will be there. Have you something you can bring?'

'I'll find something,' Ruth said. Teapots, remembering the three she had left from her collection, now distributed among the children. 'Oh, yes, I am sure I can find something.' Let's hope, she thought grimly, that he knows more about china than he does clocks.

Their meal arrived with the wine and the more she sipped and ate, the more mellow Miss Willis became. Edith, I must remember to call her, thought Ruth. She's really good company to be with and for the first time realised what a relationship she and Charmian must have had. Trying out new meals, travelling abroad – perfectly at home with each other – no wonder she missed the woman.

They sat back replete, and Edith regarded the dessert menu seriously. 'Tiramisu – oh, I love it, don't you, Ruth?'

'No, not particularly, but you have it. I can't think where you put it, you are so thin.'

'I've always eaten well and I've always been thin – it's a question of metabolisim.'

'Now, don't go all schoolmarmish on me,' Ruth said and they both laughed.

Ruth realised that she had really enjoyed her lunch with Edith Willis, more than she had expected to. She had thought it more of a charity thing – to be kind to someone who was lonely.

Well, she was lonely too, except that life in Little Astons looked more promising these days than it had in the beginning.

After lunch, they browsed in the shops, and Edith bought some postcards to send to her cousins in Scotland.

'Imagine,' she said, 'they are sisters, and they have never been outside Scotland, never been to London.'

'I had a phone call from my eldest son, Robert, yesterday,' Ruth said, as they walked home. 'He lives and works in Canada now, but he has to come to London in December and is going to spend a day with me.'

'How lovely,' Edith said. 'Is he married?'

'Yes, he is married to a lovely girl called Vanessa, and they have a thirteen-year-old son, Charles. He is over there with them but they hope he will finish his education in this country, so perhaps I shall see something of him.'

'Are they all coming?'

'No, just Robert, but this will have to do for a Christmas visit. I don't know what will happen this year.'

'You have another son?'

'Yes, Geoffrey, he is married, no children and in Dubai – and a daughter.'

'I remember her coming to the school once – she is a

teacher herself, isn't she?'

'Yes, she teaches Cookery, Food Technology, and she has two daughters. I used to see quite a lot of them when they were smaller and she also has a son.'

'So you have four grandchildren,' Edith said. 'Lucky you.'

By now they had reached Greystones.

'Thank you so much, Ruth,' Edith said. 'I have really enjoyed that. It's the best day out since I moved here.'

'Bless you,' Ruth said, 'we'll do it again.' And she walked on to Apple Tree Cottage.

As she passed Cherry Tree Cottage, she saw that the BMW was still parked outside and wondered how they were getting on. Perhaps the husband had not arrived yet.

An interesting couple, she thought, and once indoors went over to the little teapots she intended to take to the antiques evening.

Chapter Fifteen

Ruth was admiring the garden from the kitchen window. It was one of the features that had drawn her to the house. The wistaria climbing up the side wall, which the local man had cut back for the winter, the double trellis, green painted, that linked the side door to the house, the wonderful rose arbour, and the trellis walk, which was covered in various kinds of clematis both winter and summer. There was a small heather garden on the bank, which was a blaze of colour now; she had been in two minds to get rid of it and was glad she hadn't, for it bloomed almost nonstop throughout the year; various trees, a small arbutus or strawberry tree, which was so rewarding for apart from the green shiny leaves it bore white flowers like little bells, and following that the fruit. Yes, she loved the garden at Apple Tree Cottage. The climbing roses Albertine and Schoolgirl covered the front wall, and the large wooden tubs were filled with blue hydrangeas. She would fill the stone bowls with white tulips – and hoped the squirrels would keep away. It looked quite bare now – but it would not be for long. Already some things were showing signs of new growth. John would have loved it.

When the phone rang, she had an idea it might be Alice, but it was Francesca from next door.

'Ruth?'

'Yes, how are you?'

'I'm fine – settling in.'

'That's good.'

'Ruth, would you be free on Sunday evening to come round and have a drink with us? Alistair is home, and I know he would love to meet you.'

'Oh, that would be nice.'

'About six – that suit you?'

'Yes, fine, I shall look forward to that.'

And she would. Sundays could be the longest and dreariest of days – without John.

When the telephone rang again, this time it was Alice who always came straight to the point.

'When did you say Robert would be home?'

'Beginning of December, I think. It will have to be instead of a Christmas visit. He has to be in London for four days.'

'Well, when you are more certain of the date, give me a ring and I'll be over. We must celebrate, I'll cook something special. By the way, I did mean to ask you – have you seen anything of Julie?'

'Yes, I saw her last week.'

'How is she? Did you go to the wedding?'

'No, it was a very private affair – no guests – or so Julie said.'

'Doesn't sound like much fun. Is she happy?'

'Seems to be.'

'That sounds as if you have doubts?'

'No, not really, I'm just keeping my fingers crossed that it will work. It will be very strange for her.'

'Are you all right? Keeping well?'

'Yes, fine.'

'Good, good – well, take care.'

At the end of November, Janet's son David went to stay with a schoolfriend for the weekend and Janet decided to ask Eden to dinner on Saturday evening. After all, she owed him, and she quite liked the idea of seeing Eden again. So when she went to settle the account for the suit that Ralph had chosen (and very nice it was too), and one she would have chosen herself she slipped her cheque book back inside her handbag.

'Are you doing anything this Saturday, Eden?' she asked him.

He looked at her. 'Nothing much - I—'

'I wondered if you would like to come along and share dinner with me - David has gone to Cheltenham and I thought we could natter over old times.'

'Thanks, Jan, yes, what time?'

'Half seven, or to suit you, no problem,' she said, deciding to make light of the occasion.

'That's fine—'

'Half seven then,' she said. 'See you,' and left the shop on air.

Oh, to have a man around to dinner - what a treat! Now what could she get that he would appreciate? He would like a man's meal - what about roast lamb? She could buy a small leg and she and David could eat it cold or minced and dressed up Italian style - he would like that. Potatoes, carrots, mint sauce, peas and a nice apple tart to follow - one of her specials.

She followed her visit to Eden's with her usual Saturday morning stint at Greystones.

Miss Willis was a different person these days, greeting her with a smile, and telling her about her lunch with Ruth Durling at Gennaro's.

'My skin is very dry, Janet,' she said, looking in the mirror after her shampoo. 'Can you recommend something?'

'There are all sorts of things - the skin needs nourishment. Some women start very young, in their twenties even.'

'Oh, I've never found time for that,' Miss Willis said. 'Still, I can feel it is dry - flaky, almost.'

'Before I go I'll give you a list of possibles,' Janet said, 'then you can buy them yourself – the girls at the cosmetic counters are very helpful – be a trip out for you, especially if you go into Cheltenham.'

Miss Willis's face brightened. 'Yes, I could do that,' she said. 'I wonder if Ruth Durling would come with me? She might advise me, she has a very nice skin.'

'Yes, I expect she looks after it,' Janet said, but half her mind was on the evening meal.

That super French apple tart, she thought. With cream – and I must get some wine – red and white.

Miss Willis patted her hair. 'That's nice, Janet,' she said. 'Should I grow it a little?'

Janet thought. 'Well, you could,' she said. 'Be a bit softer, more of a frame for the face – of course you have good bones,' and so the session passed.

On to Mrs Bancroft who seemed to be no better. Listless might be the word, as if she had lost all interest in life. She might have a word with Mrs Woolsbridge on her way out.

Mrs Bligh was not singing this morning, but nevertheless was dressed in royal blue. Her shoes matched, high heels and pointed toes, as she teetered from the bathroom to the dressing table.

'I am going into Cheltenham this afternoon,' she said. 'I shall buy myself some new clothes.'

'A treat,' Janet said, wondering where she would put them. Her wardrobe was full already.

'They are so outdated,' Mrs Bligh complained. 'I thought I'd get a long skirt or two for winter – though goodness knows what for – there won't be any parties at Greystones. Still, my old friends might ask me.' And Janet caught a glimpse of the loneliness that might be Mrs Bligh's life in reality.

'Well, you are looking fantastic,' she said. 'And with this new rinse – Red Rum it's called, after the racehorse – you'll knock 'em cold.'

'Oh, I used to love a bob or two on the races – not like my husband – he'd put his shirt and his last quid on a horse, but I enjoyed the occasional flutter.'

Janet sighed. She had never bet on a horse in her life.

'Well, I must fly. I've got a lot of shopping to do this afternoon – see you next week.'

On the way out, she called at Mrs Woolsbridge's office to collect her monthly payment and to have a word about Mrs Bancroft.

'Mrs Bancroft doesn't seem to pick up, does she? She is so listless – did she have a shampoo this week?'

'Yes, one of the nurses did it for her. She does have a heart condition, Janet, she is bound to feel under the weather sometimes.'

'Still, it's gone on for some time. I wish I could do something for her.'

'Oh, she'll be all right,' Mrs Woolsbridge said, comfortable with the confidence of years of looking after old people.

'I might call in next week,' Janet said. 'See how she is.'

'Yes, do that,' Mrs Woolsbridge said, for once quite affable. And Janet went on her way to Cheltenham, quite concerned for Mrs Bancroft, who was her favourite client.

At half past seven, Eden arrived on Janet's doorstep, replete with a bottle of wine and a sheaf of flowers – pink lilies which, even as he brought them in, scented the little hall.

'Oh, thank you, Eden!' How long was it since she had received flowers from a man?

She led him in to the little sitting room, and disappeared into the kitchen to put them in a jug of water, hurrying back to see him settled in the big armchair.

'Now,' she smiled. 'What can I get you?'

She felt quite flustered for once, and was glad there was a pleasant smell of mint sauce and roast lamb coming from the kitchen.

'I have beer and wine, and I see you've brought red – does that mean you prefer red?'

'Yes, I do,' he said. 'That would be great. Let me open the bottle for you.'

'Oh, thanks, Eden,' and she went off to the kitchen returning with the bottle opener.

'Will you join me?' he asked.

'Please,' she said, as he opened the bottle and poured her a glass. 'Well, this is a treat.'

From where he sat he could see through into the small dining room where the table was laid for two. Shining cutlery, white napkins – very inviting, he thought.

'How has your week been?' she asked him.

'Fairly busy,' he said. 'Swings and roundabouts – you know. That's business.' He got up and took his glass to the window. 'You know, Janet, you have a great position here – that garden is a joy.'

'Yes, I love it. And we're lucky to have the fruit trees. I always liked this little lane, even when I lived at the other end of the High Street.'

He turned to her. 'Yes, you did, didn't you? You left there after you married.'

'Yes. Went to Stroud,' she said. 'With Jack.' The words came out without her volition as if to establish a fact.

'You were young,' he said.

'We all were, Eden,' she said, as they returned to the sitting room and sat down.

'Where have the years gone?'

'I often ask myself that,' he said, knowing they were making trite conversation.

'Do you regret anything?' she asked him daringly.

'Of course,' he said. 'Don't you?'

'Yes, of course. I expect everyone does. If only things had been different or if only I had married someone else.'

'Or if only I had married,' he said with a smile.

'Let's move up to date, Eden,' she said. 'What about the future? Can any of us tell? I suppose you could say we plan it but that's usually not what happens.'

'Now you're getting philosophical,' he laughed.

'I didn't know you were so learned,' and she laughed with him. 'Excuse me, I'm going to look at the oven.'

When she returned, he looked more at ease, helping himself to olives and nuts which she had remembered just in time.

'What happened between you and Jack?'

'Faults on both sides, I daresay.' She was a fair woman and was not going to give Jack away so easily. 'We should never have married but there, that's a common enough story but I don't regret my boys.'

'And you, Eden?' she looked at him. 'All these years.'

'Oh, I've had my share of girlfriends,' he said. 'But none that I ever wanted to marry or settle down with.'

'Except,' she said daringly.

'Yes,' he said, quite openly. 'Fenella.'

There was a long silence.

'I went to school with Fenella.' He stared at her. 'Of course you did, I'd forgotten.'

'We were all at school at the same time,' she said softly.

'Well, then you know, you understand,' he said.

'I don't understand how you can live all these years knowing she is married to another man and has children. I can't go along with that. I suppose you'd say I'm too much of a moralist,' she said. 'I know I am old fashioned – my sons tell me I am. And Eden,' she said, patting his arm – 'it's none of my business.'

He looked at her with something like affection. 'Anyway, it's over,' he said.

'Over!' she exploded. 'I should hope so!'

'I mean it, Jan. It hasn't been easy, for her either.'

'Oh, come on, don't expect me to be sympathetic – married to a title, a nice chap from what I hear, two lovely children, that gorgeous house – and she wants you as well – it's what's called having it all, Eden.'

He looked uncomfortable. Oh, why do I put my foot in it? Janet thought.

'She never really loved him,' he said, and she almost had to walk out of the room. The gullibility of men! She knew Fenella! She had always wanted it all.

'Yes, well, let's not talk about it and spoil our evening. I think the dinner is ready.' She disappeared into the kitchen.

She carved the meat herself, to ease off her shaking fingers and temper. Better not give him the job and she was used to carving. That Fenella! She put the sliced meat on to the plates and carried them into the dining room, following with the vegetable dishes and the gravy and the mint sauce.

'Bring your glass, Eden,' she said.

'Oh, wonderful!' he said, as if he didn't get many home-cooked meals like this. 'And you've already carved. I'm not much good,' he said. 'No experience.' And he made a face.

The meal was delicious, and Jan knew it, grateful that it had turned out such a success. The meal, anyway. She wished now she hadn't brought up the subject of Fenella but, in a way, it had cleared the air.

They were having coffee when he suddenly said: 'It is over, Jan.'

'What?' and saw his face. 'Oh, I see.'

'Yes, we met and agreed not to see each other again. She wasn't unfaithful to her husband, if that's what you thought.'

'It has nothing to do with me,' she said. 'It's your affair entirely, Eden,' but she was pleased all the same.

They sat talking of the old days and how Little Astons had changed and the time passed quickly. Glancing at his watch, Eden seemed shocked to find that it had gone midnight.

'Janet, I'd no idea it was so late. Sorry, if I've kept you up.'

She was dying to say – any time, please stay – but she got up and smiled.

'Lovely meal,' he said. 'Lovely evening, thank you, Jan, that was great.'

'Thank you for coming,' she said formally, and when he left, he kissed her lightly on the cheek.

She watched him get into his car then closed the door softly.

We must do that again, she thought.

Chapter Sixteen

On that misty Sunday evening, just after six o'clock, Ruth made her way up the drive to Cherry Tree Cottage.

The house looked so neat and trim on the outside and so newly painted, Martin's builders had certainly done a good job. The brass knocker and letter box shone and there was a large stone tub in the porch probably filled with bulbs.

Francesca answered the door, looking as elegant as ever, and took the spray of flowers Ruth handed her.

'Oh,' she said, 'thank you – how kind,' and showed Ruth into the hall, one of the most exotic interiors she had ever seen.

'Come in,' Francesca said warmly, and led her into the sitting room. The house was full of the most wonderful objets d'art, and coffee tables and painted chairs. Somehow the plain walls and curtains made a perfect backdrop for the oriental pictures and carved furniture.

'Oh, this is wonderful!' she cried, and then saw a man sitting on a large soft sofa, a walking stick by his side. He had to be one of the most handsome men Ruth had ever seen.

He sat up. 'Don't get up,' Ruth said, as he gave her a warm smile and held out his hand.

'This is Ruth, darling,' Francesca said, 'Ruth Durling from next door, Ruth, my husband, Alistair.'

'How do you do,' they both said together.

'Sit down,' Francesca said, 'while I put these in water.'

What a tragedy was the thought that went through Ruth's mind. This big handsome man brought down with multiple sclerosis. Life could be very cruel.

'How do you like your new home?' Ruth asked him with a smile.

'Love it,' he said. 'Shan't want to leave when the time comes. Still, we are doing the right thing, I know we are. Francesca's a brick you know, don't know what I'd do without her.'

Fran returned and put the flowers on the beautiful Chinese carved table.

'I can't believe it – you've transformed a Cotswold cottage,' Ruth said. 'All these lovely things.'

Fran sat down briefly while she explained. 'Alistair was a pilot with BOAC,' she said, 'and believe it or not – I was an air stewardess when we met,' and they looked across at each other. There was no doubting the love they felt and Ruth felt a lump in her throat. Such a handsome couple – but one must look on the bright side.

'So all this we collected on our travels, well, Alistair did mostly. I retired when I married and it was because he was away such a lot that I bought the business – it kept me going while he was on trips.'

Ruth was fascinated – it bore no resemblance to her house or Janet's, surprising what a change of furniture and pictures made. There were screens, painted with birds, and a wrought-iron stand dotted with lit candles which made everything so cheery – there were so many things to look at. It reminded her slightly of Julie's little sitting room, except that this was more Chinese.

'Now, what will you have – I have most things.'

'I'll join you.' Ruth said. 'Gin and tonic, wine, whatever.'

'Then let's have gin and tonic – ice and lemon?'

'Please.'

'Well, Ruth,' Alistair said, and Ruth saw what nice eyes he had but noticed the fine lines around them, and the slight pallor below. 'You too, haven't been here long – how are you liking it?'

'Love it.'

'Where were you before?'

'Cheltenham,' Ruth said. 'But we always planned to move to the Cotswolds when John retired.'

'And you are making a go of it?' He looked at her with admiration. 'Have you children?'

'Yes, three.'

'Well, that helps, doesn't it?' he asked, and Ruth wondered if he regretted not having any. But they must have led full lives.

Fran came back with the drinks on a tray and some olives and bits.

'Help yourself,' she said. 'Well, what do you think?'

'It's absolutely super,' Ruth said.

'You know, it was to have been let furnished – that was the idea but we decided to bring our stuff with us rather than have it go into storage.'

'Oh, that would have been a shame.'

'That's what we thought. To be parted from our home for six months – no, it just wasn't on – so here it is, and surprisingly it all fits in rather well. Come and look at the kitchen. Excuse us, darling.'

They walked through the hall into the kitchen, which had been completely modernised.

'Did a good job, didn't he, Martin?' Ruth admired the ultra-modern kitchen, small though, with everything to hand a woman would need.

They went back to the sitting room passing the closed door of the dining room. 'I won't show you the dining room,' Fran explained, 'for I have a bed in there just in case Alistair doesn't feel he can make the stairs. So far he is okay but you never know.'

'Fine kitchen, isn't it?' Alistair asked on their return.

'Excellent, he's remembered everything.'

'Oh, he's a poppet,' Fran said, which certainly wasn't a

word Ruth would have used to describe him. 'He's been such a friend, hasn't he, Alistair?'

Alistair nodded. 'He's a great chap,' he said. 'Fran went to school with him.' He grinned.

She grinned back. 'Yes, I did but he was one of the big boys, and he used to protect me from the rough boys.' She smiled. 'You've met him, haven't you, Ruth?'

Ruth had the grace to blush. 'Yes, briefly,' she said. 'I went into the shop once.'

'And doesn't he have some lovely things? It was a sad day for him when Stella walked out.'

Ruth remained silent, feigning ignorance.

'His wife, you know, she left him this year but good riddance, I say.'

'Darling,' Alistair remonstrated.

'Well . . .'

'Tell me, Ruth, what did your husband do? Has he been gone long?'

'No, last year. He was at the Foreign Office.'

'And you decided to change your lifestyle completely?'

'Yes, I taught in Cheltenham but I was due to retire anyway, and I was glad to – I'd had enough.'

'I can imagine that teaching might be rather hard work,' he said, and helped himself to olives and biscuits.

'Yes, it had its moments,' Ruth said. 'Nothing like as exotic as the life you two must have led.'

'Well, it too had its moments.'

'It always sounds so exciting flying round the world, seeing places.'

'It is, there's nothing like it.' You could tell how much he missed it.

'Anyway, what have you been finding to do?' Fran obviously wanted to change the subject.

'Not a lot really – not enough, anyway. I've joined the Red Cross one afternoon a week but I need to find more to do. Once you get settled perhaps you can give me some tips?'

'I too will have to be occupied. The shop has taken up most of my time but in any case we are only here for six months. Alistair is able to get about at the moment but that could change and we are determined to beat this thing, aren't we darling? Not let it get the better of us. That's why we are having the bungalow built – we couldn't have managed those stairs to the flat above the shop for ever.'

'No, and this is great,' Alistair said heartily.

You had to hand it to them, Ruth thought, in the face of adversity they were making the best of a bad job.

After another half an hour, during which they talked of many things, Ruth left. What a nice couple. And it was true, you could always find people worse off than yourself.

Everything happened at once on that misty first of December: the odd job man arrived to saw down a stump of a tree at the bottom of the garden, the electricity man arrived to see to the washing machine which was not working properly and the phone rang, almost all at the same time.

The phone was Robert, phoning from Canada. 'Ma, sorry to disappoint you but there has been a change of plan.'

'Oh, Rob.'

'I am not coming to London after all but guess what? I'm being posted to Washington.'

'Oh, is that good?' It sounded like it from his tone.

'Yes, wonderful. Vanessa is pleased, too, so it means—'

'That you won't be over – never mind, no good saying I am not disappointed and I know Alice will be too.'

'Yes, I'll phone her later.'

'But congratulations, Rob.'

'Thank you, and we've had an idea. We're moving in ten days' time, so why not come over for Christmas – or even New Year, if Christmas is too soon.'

'Oh, I don't know, Rob, there's—'

'Well, I'll leave you to think about it – in the meantime—'

'And Rob, congratulations, and love to Vanessa.'

She put down the phone to find the washing-machine man waiting patiently and quickly deflected her thoughts to him. 'I'm sorry, that was my son from Canada. Now . . .'

She sat later in the kitchen – what a disappointment – she had looked forward so much to Robert coming over. But it couldn't be helped and he sounded pleased at his new appointment. He had followed his father into the Foreign Office, and it was true, you never knew where you would be sent next, but going for Christmas! She wasn't sure she wanted to – besides, they wouldn't have been in the house five minutes – oh, she would think about it later. In the meantime a cup of tea for the man in the kitchen and another for the jobbing gardener. She hoped to get out in time to go to Dolly's, where they would be discussing plans for the Christmas Fair. She would telephone Alice this evening.

She did eventually make it after a hasty lunch and walked leisurely to Dolly Lister's house where she found them all much as usual, busy sorting pieces for patchwork.

'Oh, Ruth dear, sit yourself down.'

A lively argument followed about the pros and cons of the Christmas Fair, the venue, and the date, which passed a good half an hour.

Then they started talking eagerly about the forthcoming so-called *Antiques Road Show*, which was proving to be more popular than they could have imagined. Right on their doorstep . . .

'Will you be coming, Ruth?'

'Yes, of course,' she laughed, 'I wouldn't miss it for the world.'

She thought on the way home, it was not quite what she imagined – sewing for the Red Cross, however, it did someone some good, and passed a few hours. Where was her promise to herself to improve her learning skills, take up another language? Perhaps she should buy a computer – but the thought scared her. It wasn't as if she was keen on the idea. But you had to keep up with the times, if you wanted to stay youthful.

Janet Foster was toying with the idea of giving her notice in up at Astons Manor. What had been an interesting little job had now turned into a bit of a bore and she would not argue that her talk with Eden Brook had finally caused her to make up her mind.

She found herself now disapproving more than ever of Fenella, her one-time friend. True, she now no longer saw her on a friendly basis and, on the rare occasions when they did meet up at the manor, Fenella had little to say to her.

No wonder, thought Janet. She felt quite hostile.

The decision was made for her when a few days later Eden telephoned to say that he had been to a Rotary Club meeting the night before and the subject of Luigi's sale of his hairdressing business had cropped up.

'He didn't mention a price?'

'No but said he would rather sell it without an agent if he could and we talked about the possibilities of that and the drawbacks – otherwise nothing.'

'Thanks, Eden,' she said.

She would go and see Luigi at the first opportunity. But first, she had something to do.

She telephoned the housekeeper at Astons Manor and asked for an appointment. It was fixed for that afternoon, and Janet drove herself up to the house, looking around with approbation at the beautiful gardens surrounding the house.

No doubt about it, Fenella had enough to keep her occupied without keeping Eden dangling on a string.

The business was easily conducted and concluded. It was arranged that she would leave immediately since the house closed down to visitors from now until May. The interview was amicable and Janet drove away with a feeling that she was pleased it had come to an end.

Now perhaps she could get on with realising her dream to own Luigi's hairdressing salon. Of course, if it transpired that it was too much money, then that was that.

On her way home, she stopped at the florist's and bought some pink roses for Mrs Bancroft. The old lady had been on her mind lately, and she knew she would be pleased with a call.

She was in bed, her book upside down on the coverlet, but she was not asleep, although her eyes were closed; she opened them and looked at Janet with sheer pleasure.

'Here,' Jan said, handing her the roses.

'Oh, how kind of you, they're lovely.'

'Not much scent – but they look nice,' Janet said. 'I'll put them in water for you.'

She found a small vase, filled it with water, and put the flowers on Mrs Bancroft's bedside table.

She sat down on the chair next to the bed. 'How have you been?'

'Tired, mostly,' Mrs Bancroft said. 'Can't seem to rouse myself.'

'It's the time of year,' Janet said.

'And what have you been up to?' Mrs Bancroft said. 'How are those boys of yours?'

'They're fine. Ralph is doing well – I've seen no more of the girlfriend, in fact he hasn't been home for a bit, and David – well, it's the football season so I don't see much of him. But he's a good lad and does his homework, so I can't complain. Someone has cleaned your windows,' she smiled. 'Nothing like clean windows, is there?'

'Yes, a man came – I can't see so well – my eyes are not what they were.'

Janet looked around the walls, at the embroidered pictures and paintings, a few watercolours.

'You are surrounded by lovely things,' she said, and found herself looking hard again at the small oil painting of boats on a river. She was quite fascinated by it: the river, the skies, the old ships with their sails.

'That *is* lovely,' she said. 'I could look at that all day . . . Where is it?'

Mrs Bancroft turned to look at the picture.

'Amsterdam,' she said. 'Do you know it – have you been there?'

Janet shook her head. 'No,' she said.

Mrs Bancroft was lost in thought. 'There is a story attached to that picture. It was painted by a man called Ludolf Bakhuyzen – a Dutchman, famous for his oil paintings of Amsterdam and the sea. My husband, whose family originally came from Holland, had a friend called Dr Anton Dressmann, who was a great collector – he died not long ago – and he knew how fond my husband was of Dutch paintings. Anyway, to cut a long story short my husband bought it – it was the first piece of real art that he bought. He loved it, and so do I.' She turned to look at Janet. 'When I die, I want you to have it.' It was said so matter-of-factly, that Janet gasped.

Mrs Bancroft put a hand over hers. 'It is for you. No one else in the family has ever been remotely interested.'

Janet was shocked. 'Oh, you mustn't say that,' she said. 'And you're not going anywhere. You're going to get better and even get out again, I mean it.'

Mrs Bancroft's eyes filled with tears. 'You are a good girl,' she said.

'Shall I read to you for a bit.'

'Please, dear.'

After five minutes, Janet closed the book. Mrs Bancroft was asleep and Janet tiptoed out of the room.

Everything was geared up to the Antiques Evening. It was quite the most notable event Little Astons had had for a long time, not since the Coronation Party in 1953.

The village hall was taken over, the platform rigged up with pots of flowers, and a table set for the welcoming of the two men and two women from Rokebys who were coming down from London to run the affair.

Tickets had been sold, sold out, for there was a limited number of persons who could fill the hall.

Ruth had definitely decided that she would take one of the little teapots – one she had had for many years. She had started collecting teapots when she was a young woman and had built up a collection of fifty-three. She picked up the one she had in mind. It wasn't the oldest or the most attractive. Some of the Chinese ones, and the special china ones – sometimes with a stand, sometimes with an inner tealeaf strainer – had been unique, but this little brown teapot was special.

She remembered it as if it were yesterday. She and John had had a fierce argument – over what she couldn't now remember, but he had flung off to the office, and she had gone sulkily to school, both of them furious with the other.

That evening when he came home, her anger had subsided, and he came in sheepishly with a small parcel. Inside was a teapot – she couldn't say it was the prettiest thing she had ever seen. It was, in fact, studio pottery, which didn't go with her porcelain collection but there was something about the little pot that she took to. She remembered how they had hugged each other, and later she had looked up its history.

It was, as she had suspected, a Cardew teapot, probably produced sometime in the early twentieth century, and she learned that Cardew had been a pupil of the famous Bernard Leach, since when he had set up his own studio in Gloucestershire, which was probably why it had been found locally.

So it stood among her collection, simply because it was a country pottery type of teapot and she loved it because John had bought it for her. She had kept it, and now she wrapped it in tissue paper, carefully placed it in a bag, and prepared to go to the village hall. Well, Mr Martin

Amesbury, she said to herself, let's see if you know what this is – expert on Chinese porcelain and English china …

She was to meet Edith and pick her up at Greystones, and Edith brought with her a small Victorian portrait locket which her elderly Scottish aunt had left her. It was a pretty thing and very wearable, except that Ruth could hardly imagine Edith wearing it, it was not her kind of thing.

The hall was packed when they arrived and tables had been set up for dealing with each type of antique. At the back of the hall, several pieces of small furniture stood, and paintings. She had been told it had taken quite a lot of organising to arrange all this.

Six people sat on the platform, in the centre Martin Amesbury, and now he rapped on the table with a small gavel and asked for quiet. He spoke of the arrangements that had been made, and would people please go to their allotted tables where notices would tell them if they were at the right table; would they queue in an orderly manner – and so on, and she had to admit he did it very well.

The evening had begun, and Ruth took her place in the china and porcelain queue, while Edith went over to jewellery. It was fascinating to watch the experts evaluating the items, and to listen to what they had to say.

Martin Amesbury had taken his seat and saw the first member of the queue and Ruth had to admit grudgingly that he did an excellent job. They were mostly women, she noticed, proffering their items of interest, and there were several of these. She listened intently to what he had to say, and there was much laughter all around the hall as people were either pleased at the verdict given or shocked to think their item was of no value.

When it came to Ruth's turn, she took her seat at the chair beside him, and he looked up and smiled. 'Ah, Mrs Durling,' he said, 'we meet again.'

'Yes,' she said, wanting to add 'sir' as though she were back at school.

He unwrapped the little teapot to expose it in all its glory – not a delicate piece of porcelain, but a sturdy practical little teapot, which however had a charm of its own.

He smiled at her. 'Not my usual thing,' he said, and she could have hit him, 'but, nevertheless it has an exciting look about it.'

She frowned. Exciting – that's the last thing she would have called it. 'Do you know what it is?'

She was not going to stick her neck out, so she shook her head.

'It is a Cardew teapot, made around 1930 by Michael Cardew and followers of his work will immediately recognise the decoration. He revived seventeenth- and eighteenth-century styles and techniques, such as slip trailing, to create pieces that sit well alongside English country furniture. He was apprenticed to Bernard Leach from 1923 before he set up his own pottery in Winchcombe quite near here. Value, well, I should say around six hundred pounds.' Ruth gasped.

'Surprised, Mrs Durling?'

She took a breath. 'Well, yes, I am,' In more ways than one, she wanted to add. 'Thank you very much.' He wrapped it gently and handed it to her; looking up into her eyes, there was no mistaking the gleam of wry amusement in his very blue ones.

Cheeky devil, she thought, walking away with her treasure – and a frisson of pleasure ran through her. You are sixty-two years old, Ruth Durling – what is it with you and that man?

She walked over towards the jewellery stand, where Edith was three away from being seen, and stood and watched the procedure. As Edith drew nearer to being seen, she stood by her side.

'Ah,' the valuer said, picking up Edith's necklace. 'A

very pretty thing. Victorian, of course, the Victorians were very fond of sentimental jewellery, and this is no exception. This contains the portrait of a lady in a pear-shaped mount, topped by a ribbon bow, studied with tiny diamonds and the fine herringbone chain has a half-pearl clasp. The portrait is not of great value on its own but this makes it a very affordable piece of jewellery. Is it a family piece?' he asked Edith.

'Yes, it was left to me by a Scottish aunt, but I do not know its history,' Edith said.

'Then I am sure you wish to keep it for sentimental value but I should say it would be worth something like two hundred pounds.'

'Goodness!' Edith said, quite taken aback. 'I thought it was a trinket.'

'Anything but,' the valuer said. 'It is charming – and I am sure you will enjoy wearing it.'

'Well!' Edith said. 'Can you believe it – I only brought it because I hadn't anything else. What about your teapot?'

'I can hardly believe it – he put a value of six hundred on it.'

'Six hundred for that wee teapot?' Edith said. 'What a nonsense it all is. But I might even wear my locket – I've quite taken a fancy to it.'

'Oh, I would,' Ruth said enthusiastically. 'It's lovely.'

They walked round looking at all the other stands and spent an enjoyable evening together. Later, they wandered home together, Ruth leaving Edith at Greystones.

'Oh, I did enjoy that,' Edith Willis said. 'I can't thank you enough for your friendship, Ruth. It has made such a difference to my life.'

'Mine, too,' laughed Ruth, and thought, she's not such a bad old stick. It takes all sorts, after all.

Tucked up in bed with her book, she closed it and switching off the light, settled down.

What an extraordinary man he is – Martin Amesbury, she thought, going over the events of the evening. He has a sense of humour, that's apparent – and wondered not for the first time what it had to do with her.

That little teapot – wouldn't John be pleased. Altogether she had spent a very interesting evening . . .

Chapter Seventeen

'Going where?' Alice said.

'Washington – for Christmas.'

'You have to be joking,' Alice said.

'Robert telephoned me and asked me over.'

'But they've only been there five minutes.'

'Well, I'm not—'

'I should think not! Travelling about in the Christmas rush – you're not a teenager. Besides, the children would miss you – they never see you these days.'

'I know, that's one of the reasons I am not going – it's too soon—'

'Exactly, you'll come to us as usual, I hope, and what about Geoff? Isn't he coming back from Dubai?'

'I don't know, I haven't heard—'

'No – go in the spring – it's warmer then. Washington in December – ugh, can't bear to think of it.'

So much for Washington, Ruth thought, but then she had decided not to go anyway. The timing was wrong.

'Got to go. My class is making small Christmas puddings – I will have forty-two to judge.'

Rather you than me, Ruth thought, never having excelled at cooking. But Alice was dedicated.

Janet had an appointment with Luigi for ten-thirty on Thursday.

She paid a lot of attention to her hair and make-up before setting off in her black trouser suit and cream cashmere scarf.

She liked Luigi. Having worked for him for a couple of days a week, one of them his day off, she had got to know him quite well, but she had never seriously discussed the purchase of his lease on the salon.

His father had been a prisoner of war in the Second World War, and Luigi a child when it ended. He had followed his father into the business he had built up after the war, married and had two sons himself, and a bevy of daughters, all of whom had gone back to Italy. He couldn't wait to join them – it was only his father's business that had kept him here so long.

He liked Janet Foster and had known her husband. They had come to see him soon after they married to look into the possibility of taking over his salon. But he hadn't wanted to sell it then. Now, with changed circumstances, he knew the time had come for him to return to his beloved homeland, the country which he had never really lived in except for holidays since he was a small child.

As for Janet, she was honest, hard working, and an excellent hairdresser. He would have liked her to work in the shop in those days but she had gone off to Spain with that handsome husband of hers. Luigi could have told her that it wouldn't work. An eye for the ladies – that was Jack Foster.

It was a small establishment and Luigi knew that he could do with larger premises, he was so popular. But the timing was wrong – he was too old, and he now waited for her in the small kitchen which also served as an office. All his money went on the business, and he had an 85-year lease. He also knew that he could sell it over and over again and there were many prospective purchasers. Of course, you had to put business first, but he favoured Janet. She deserved some luck. But she would have to pay the right price. He couldn't afford to give it away.

'Ah, Janet, my dear,' he said, his balding head shining under the lamps in the salon, the curly grey fringe like a frill round the back of his head. 'Come through, my dear.'

'Luigi,' Janet said, smiling at him, and the thought went through Luigi's head as it had often done, that he wished he were a younger man. Since the death of his wife some years earlier, he had been lonely, but if he married again, God willing, he knew it would be to an Italian lady.

Janet's eyes swept the salon, noticing the new receptionist, a girl of about eighteen with a mass of red hair, very smart but no diamond studs or tattooing. Oh, I would love to own this salon! she thought.

'Sit down, Janet,' Luigi said. 'How're keeping?'

'I'm fine, thank you. And you?'

He sat down opposite her. 'Very well. Looking forward to getting this settled. I've been a lifetime here.'

'I know – it will be a wrench,' Janet said. 'But you've a lot to look forward to – seeing your family again.'

His dark eyes glowed. 'Yes, that's true.'

There were some papers in a folder on the table, and now he opened it.

'We've fixed a price, my solicitor and I,' he said, 'and I guess that is the most important thing, eh?'

'Yes, it is in my case,' Janet said.

'Well,' he referred to his notes. 'I'll get to the point. To include goodwill, fixtures and fittings, and of course, if you remember, there is a flat over the shop. I'll take you up there if you are interested. When we had the family at home, my wife and I bought a little house out Stowe way, but since the children moved away and my wife died, I've been living over the shop. It has three bedrooms, a bathroom, kitchen and sitting room – you could always let that – bring in a bit of revenue.'

Janet had forgotten that.

'Lock stock and barrel,' Luigi said 'with an eighty-five-year lease—' He named a figure that was way beyond Janet's possibilities. He saw her face drop with disappointment. He had thought it would be too much for her. He had come as low as he could and the place was worth it.

'Too much, my dear?'

Janet nodded.

'No chance of a bank loan?'

Janet shook her head. 'No, for various reasons,' and thought of the boys' education. She could not afford to plunge the family into debt. Of course, on the other hand she would earn more, be more secure – but no. Better face it. It had been worth a try.

She stood up. 'No point in my hanging around, Luigi, it's way off my beat.' She smiled ruefully. 'But it was worth a try.'

He held out his hand. 'Okay Janet. I'm sorry too, I would have liked you to have it. It won't go on the open market until after Christmas in fact, but if I get any private offers I will keep in touch, just in case you change your mind—'

'My mind is made up,' she laughed. 'It's my bank manager that's the trouble.' She shook his hand.

'Good luck,' he said, 'and if I don't see you, happy Christmas. I'm going back to Italy for Christmas but not until the day before Christmas Eve.'

'Have a great time,' Janet said, and walked slowly down the High Street towards Notcutts Lane.

Once home she went to her little desk and took out her private papers, juggling the accounts, bills, demands, mortgage. Of course, she could sell the little house and move upstairs into the flat over the salon, but knew she wouldn't. She wouldn't inflict that on the boys. They loved their home and their garden and they had had enough disruption in their young lives. No, she would stay in Notcutts Lane. Accepting a situation was half the battle. It was ridiculous to pursue a dream that was just not possible.

She would have to find another job to fill in her Thursdays now she had left Astons Manor, and the new owners of the salon might not want to employ her. She'd worry about that tomorrow – no good fretting about it now.

Later in the day, she telephoned Eden Brook. 'Hi, Eden, Janet.'

'Janet, how did you get on?'

'No joy,' she said. 'What I thought really, and I'm not surprised, the place is worth it.'

'Would you like me to come round for a drink, I'll bring a bottle of wine?'

'Oh, would you? Thanks Eden, don't bother about the wine, I have some.'

Oh, how good it was to have a man to talk to.

She opened a packet of cheese biscuits and a few nuts and raisins, got two glasses out on a tray, and set them on the table together with a bottle of wine.

It was almost six o'clock and David wouldn't be in until seven.

She pulled the curtains – how dark it got this time of year – and threw another log on to the fire. That was the good thing about a fire – it was so cheerful.

Upstairs, she washed, made up her face, and brushed her lustrous hair – what we do for a man, she thought, and went downstairs to greet Eden.

Eden kissed her lightly on the cheek on entering, and presented her with a bunch of beautiful pink roses.

'Oh, you shouldn't have, but come through.'

'My word,' and he rubbed his hands together when he saw the fire. 'A real one.'

'Yes, I like a fire – it's cosy . . . red – white?'

'Red please.'

'I did open it,' she said, and poured him a glass, then a glass for herself, and sat down opposite him.

He took a sip. 'Well, what's the figure?'

'Not bad,' he said when she told him. 'All things considered. It's a busy little salon, and there is that flat over the top, that'd bring in quite a bit, Jan.'

'I know, I've thought of that but I'd be stretched to the limit with an extra bank loan. Perhaps I am being too ambitious.'

'No help from your ex?' he suggested.

'I wouldn't want that,' she reprimanded him.

'Sorry, well, you tried.'

'Yes. I've looked at it all ways but, no, best accept it. Have a crisp.'

They stared into the fire, then he turned to her. 'Janet, don't be offended but—'

She looked up startled, eyebrows raised.

'Um, would you consider taking a loan from me? You could pay me back – it would be purely and simply a business transaction. The shop's doing well and I have some savings ...'

She was shocked. 'Oh, Eden! I'm sorry, thank you, but I couldn't do that.'

He looked a little embarrassed himself. 'I'm sorry if I—'

'No, not at all, it was very kind of you but I'll live with it. It was a pipe dream and would mean probably biting off more than I could chew.'

She brightened up. 'Well, you're busy then – at work? The shops in the village seem to be. Everything looks so nice, decorated and without the tourists.'

'Yes, I agree. I've lots of Christmas orders.'

'What do you do at Christmas? Go to your sister's?'

'Sometimes, not this year.'

'If you're at a loose end, you can share our Christmas dinner – there will be just me and the boys,' she said impulsively and was astonished to see his face light up.

'Really, Jan? I would like that.'

And he meant it. She sat staring into the fire and he guessed she was probably thinking about her visit to Luigi's. Pity about her marriage though. It wouldn't have been Jan's fault, he was sure. Jack was a womaniser – always had been – and he could never understand why Janet didn't see it. She had been the prettiest girl in the village – yes, even more pretty than Fenella. Where Fenella had been classically beautiful, Janet was warm and pretty – and fun.

She looked up and caught him looking to her.

'You have lovely hair, Janet,' he said, causing her to feel slightly embarrassed.

'Thank you,' she said, her voice low.

'It's natural, isn't it?' he asked and she burst out laughing.

'What did you think – it was dyed, permed?'

Now it was his turn. 'No, I mean it's always looked like that, ever since you were at school.'

'Yes, I'm not one for changes,' she said.

'I didn't mean that,' he said seriously and Janet thought he wouldn't get an award for knowing how to compliment a woman.

'I mean, no grey hair.'

'Not yet,' she said, 'but I suppose I can look forward to that. I'm getting on – thirty-nine.'

'Two or three years younger than I am,' he said.

How did we get into this conversation, Janet wondered. After all this time?

'Do you get lonely, Jan? I mean, do you miss Jack?'

'Yes, to the first question, no to the second,' Janet laughed. She was about to offer him a top up, but thought he might think she was encouraging him. So she sat still, her glass half empty beside her and held out the dish of mixed nuts.

He got up and refilled her glass and his own. 'How is David doing at school?'

'Reasonably well, he's not as bright as Ralph, but he'll get by. I'm not worried about him.'

He suddenly got up and moved over to the fire, standing with his back to her. 'I expect you'll think I'm mad,' he said. 'After all these years,' he added, turning to face her.

She raised her face, her brown eyes questioning him.

'I mean, we get on together, don't we? We've known each other for years.' Her heart started to race, but she was speechless.

'Do you think – I mean, could we make a go of it? You and me? Isn't it a waste of two people's lives as we are? Or am I jumping the gun. Perhaps you have—'

She shook her head. She couldn't have been more shocked. Then common sense took over. 'You mean shack up together?'

At her choice of words, he frowned. 'You mean – live together. Set up home together.'

'Well—' And suddenly she was furious.

Here was a man who had carried a torch for another woman for almost all his adult life. They were both young, it was true, young enough to start again but she had the boys – what would they think of the suggestion? True, Ralph was almost grown up but – David?

Besides – yes, it was tempting to have a man around – but women had passed that stage. They no longer needed men – a man in your life meant extra work, giving up your time to him, cooking for him, washing his socks – you would really need to be fond of him to do that. She had been there, done that – and look where it had got her. Mind – Eden was a different kettle of fish. Could she ever love him? Was he really fond of her, or would it be a relationship of convenience?

He was watching her.

'That set-up is not my style, Eden,' she said at last. 'I am one of the old-fashioned ones.' And she laughed to ease the tension. 'I was brought up proper,' she added, just as David came pushing through the front door, his face red from running, and stopped dead as soon as he saw Eden.

'Hello, Mr Brook,' he said.

'Hi, David.'

'I've been round at Tom's,' David said. 'Can I go to his house for lunch on Sunday?'

'Sunday?' Janet queried.

'It's Tom's birthday,' David said.

'Oh, well, in that case ...' Turning to look at Eden, she saw a smile in his eyes.

What sort of a dad would he make? She put the thought away from her.

Eden made as if to go, but Janet forestalled him.

'Don't go,' she said. 'I'll just get David's tea out of the oven – back in a moment, help yourself to wine.'

When she returned to the sitting room Eden was sitting back relaxed on the sofa, browsing through one of David's sporting magazines.

It was nice to have a man in the house, Janet thought, as she opened the door and saw Eden sitting there.

'Right,' she said.

'Jan, if David is going to Tom's on Sunday, why don't we go out to lunch?'

Now *that*, she thought, I really would enjoy.

And so the preparations for Christmas went on in Little Astons.

A week before, with festivities at their height, Ruth answered the door to find Francesca standing there with a bunch of pink roses.

'For me? Oh, thank you, Fran, how lovely. Come in.'

'No, I won't stop, I have to get back. Alistair hasn't been too well today, and I want him to have an early night. Tomorrow some of his old pilot friends are coming to lunch and I think he's got excited.'

'Very likely,' Ruth smiled. 'Now, don't forget, if there is anything I can do – I'm not going away or anything – or only up to Alice's, if you feel like coming in for a drink, you and Alistair, it's open house. And thank you for the lovely roses.'

'Oh, you are sweet,' Fran said. 'I won't want to leave here when the times comes.'

Ruth watched her walking up the narrow drive, and saw

the lamp post light up her shining hair. Oh, how brave they were, those two. She closed the door quietly and went to put the roses in water.

Chapter Eighteen

Janet arrived at Greystones to find Christmas decorations everywhere. Many of them were from before Mrs Woolsbridge's time, but nevertheless, someone had been busy hanging them. There was holly behind the pictures and a small Christmas tree decorated with lights - imagine, lit up during the day, Mrs W must be feeling generous and garlands of greenery hung over the stairs, altogether it made a welcome display.

She changed as usual, putting on her white coat. How would she find Mrs Bancroft today ... She had left the bringing of gifts until nearer Christmas Eve.

She dropped the library books upstairs to the old lady, who seemed unaware that any festivities were going on. As long as she had her books she was quite happy. Thank God she still has her eyesight, thought Janet.

On the first floor, she called in on Miss Willis, putting off, she knew, confrontation with Mrs Bancroft, for she had a feeling that Mrs Bancroft was not long for this world, and dreaded finding her worse, especially at Christmas - but what did it mean to her?

Miss Willis was in a very good mood. She had decided, she said, to go to Scotland for Christmas which she had not visited for twenty years.

'I have a distant cousin of my mother's in Edinburgh - she must be in her eighties now, and I wrote to her. It's time I went, and I shall look forward to that.'

'How will you go?' Janet asked.

'By train, dear,' Edith Willis said. 'I am going the day after tomorrow and will probably stay for New Year. Can't miss a Scottish New Year, you know . . .'

What a change had come over her, Janet thought, really since Ruth Durling had arrived on the scene.

'So what shall we have – a shampoo today?'

'Please dear. Let me take off my necklace – I've taken to wearing it.'

'How pretty,' Janet said. 'You should wear it all the time.'

'Well, not all the time – mostly evenings, but I put it on today to show you. It's an heirloom and—' she stressed – 'worth a lot of money.'

'I should think so,' Janet said, eyeing it closely, and it was indeed quite striking. She laid it down gently on the dressing table. 'Here we go,' she said.

When she left, Miss Willis gave her a tablet of lavender soap.

'Oh, how kind,' Janet said, and kissed her swiftly on the cheek.

'I would have waited but I am off in two days.' Her eyes positively shone.

'Now you take care,' Janet said. 'You'll get a taxi to the station and change at Paddington for the train going north.'

Edith Willis smiled. 'Yes, dear,' she said. 'I shall be fine.'

'Have a wonderful time,' Janet said. She might have been talking to a different person.

Now for Mrs Bancroft. There was no change in Mrs Bancroft, although her eyes lit up when she saw Janet.

'Ah, my dear, I have been looking forward to your coming,' and attempted to lift herself into a sitting position.

Janet rushed to help her. 'There, is that comfy?'

'You're a good girl, Janet.'

'Do you think you will get downstairs for Christmas? It looks very festive.'

'I'm sure. Mrs Woolsbridge makes an effort at Christmas – you have to hand it to her.'

'So she should,' Janet said.

'Now, how did the visit from your daughter go? How is she?' she saw the frown come over Mrs Bancroft's face.

'It is good of her to come, she is busy and she had to come all the way from Manchester – she was working there this week.'

And that won't do her any harm, thought Janet, realising that she really had it in for this daughter of Mrs Bancroft's.

'Is there anything you would like especially?' she asked. 'I shall be going into Cheltenham in a day or two.'

'No, thank you dear, I have my cards, and I usually send the grandchildren money. It's safer that way, then they can buy what they want.'

'Now what are we going to do about your hair. Do you fancy a shampoo? You might feel better after that – eh?'

'No, leave it, Janet. Can you come in a day or two – just so as I get it done before Christmas?'

'Yes, I could – Thursday – how about that?'

'Yes, that would be fine. I'm sorry to be a nuisance.'

'You're not a nuisance,' Janet said, and bending over her, kissed her on her cheek. 'Now, you rest there and I'll see you later. You're sure you don't want anything from the shops?'

'No, Rose will get me anything if I do.' Then she seemed to remember. 'What are you doing for Christmas, Janet? Are your boys going to be home?'

'Yes, great, isn't it?'

'Yes, wonderful.'

Janet heaved a sigh – poor Mrs Bancroft. Now for Mrs Bligh.

But Mrs Bligh was sitting at the dressing table, very much the worse for wear. Her cheeks were tear stained and her eyes red and puffy.

'Now, what on earth is the matter?' Janet asked.

'I always feel miserable at Christmas since Bob died - I mean, it's sad, isn't it? Christmas, I mean.'

'Of course not - it's a lovely time,' Janet said, although she knew what Mrs Bligh meant. 'What are you doing for Christmas? Staying here?'

'I was,' Mrs Bligh said, 'but I can't bear the thought of it.'

'Then book into a swish hotel,' Janet urged her. 'There's still time.'

Mrs Bligh brightened considerably. 'Do you think I could? It's not too late? After all, I can afford it.'

'Well then, do it!' Janet said. 'You'll feel heaps better. I'll give you a special rinse today.'

'Oh, will you, Janet?' Mrs Bligh was getting brighter by the minute. 'Let me tell you what I bought - look in the wardrobe, dear, you can't mistake it.'

You certainly couldn't. It was pink, knee length in front, the back falling to the ankles, and encrusted with faux diamonds, two narrow shoulder straps and very décolleté.

Janet swallowed. 'Oh, how unusual!'

'Get it out and I'll show you.'

It must have cost a fortune Janet realised as soon as she saw the label. 'I bet you'll look smashing in that,' she said.

'Do you think so?' Already Mrs Bligh's cheeks were flushed with excitement. 'It's the very latest thing, the girl said.'

'You'll knock 'em cold,' Janet said, in Mrs Bligh's idiom.

So with Mrs Bligh quite cheered up, and a smile on her face as she thought of Mrs Bligh with her pink dress and red hair, Janet went on her way.

*

Ruth was in the kitchen when the telephone rang.

'What is Julie's new name – and address?' It was Alice.

'Wait, and I'll get it for you. It seemed so strange to write to her as Mrs Stringer,' Ruth said flicking over her phone book. 'She is now Mrs Albert Stringer, 6 Fountain Court, Park Lane, W1.'

'Half a mo,' Alice was writing it down. 'Have you seen her yet?'

'No, but I phoned her old flat twice, and got through to her new address in Park Lane – got it from directory enquiries, and a male voice said, "She is not here".'

'Perhaps they are away?'

'Possibly, her life has changed so much.'

'Well, the children are looking forward to seeing you. They want to come over to see Apple Tree Cottage.'

'Lovely. Any time,' Ruth said, cheered at the thought.

'Everything all right?'

'Yes, fine.'

'Take care, see you then.'

Ruth had a thought. She would telephone Julie again at both addresses – it had been so long since she had spoken to her. She would have time before calling for Edith Willis, for they were going out to a Christmas lunch together at Gennaro's.

No. No joy there. A woman's voice at the Park Lane address said Mrs Stringer was resting and did not want to be disturbed.

Resting . . . Julie. That seemed odd. She mustn't make a mountain out of a molehill, but take care to remember that Julie was now a married woman with obligations. She had another life completely.

Edith was waiting for her in the camel coat and matching scarf, and the Homburg-type hat pulled down over her face because of the wind.

'Oh, this was a really good idea, Ruth,' she said. 'I've been looking forward to it all week.'

'When do you go up to Scotland?'

'Saturday. I can't wait! What about you?'

'I shall drive over to Alice's on Christmas morning – early – in time to see the start of the festivities,' Ruth said. I probably won't recognise my grandson – he grows taller every time I see him.'

'I didn't realise you had another grandson.'

'Yes, Alice's son. I never see the other one. He is in Washington now but hopefully I will go over before long.'

By now they had reached Gennaro's, decorated for the festive season and warm and welcoming. They ordered wine and decided to have the traditional Christmas lunch of roast turkey with all the trimmings.

Edith sat facing the diners in the restaurant, while Ruth faced the window. Sipping their wine, they toasted each other, then Edith leaned forward and spoke to Ruth. 'We have a fellow diner – over there. You can't see him but the man who did the valuation at Rokeby's.'

Who could she mean but Martin Amesbury?

From that moment on, Ruth felt distinctly – aware – of him. Of course he dined out sometimes. Why not? He had no wife now ... she wondered what he did at Christmas. His daughter was in South Africa, someone had said. Would she come over to see her father?

They were just finishing their dessert when Ruth felt a light hand on her shoulder and, looking up, saw Martin Amesbury smiling down at her.

'Mrs Durling – Ruth, isn't it?'

Ruth, her face flushed, partly from wine, partly from sheer embarrassment, smiled. 'Ah, Mr Amesbury.'

'Martin,' he said.

'My friend, Edith Willis – Martin Amesbury,' she said, 'you remember?'

Edith beamed. 'Of course, the antiques man. The teapot man,' she said. 'How do you do?'

'I'd like to wish you ladies a very happy Christmas,' he said.

‘Thank you and to you too,’ they both said, and he went on his way.

‘Charming man,’ Edith said.

You can say that again, Ruth thought.

Everything was set for Christmas Day lunch at Plum Tree Cottage. From the kitchen came the smell of roast turkey and cranberry sauce, roast potatoes and roast parsnips, green vegetables, while candles set about the dining table lent it a festive air. The fire burned brightly in the hearth.

Eden was seeing to the drinks, while the boys were upstairs in their rooms sorting out their Christmas gifts, mostly items of clothing and books and magazines.

‘Want any help, Jan? Here, let me,’ he offered, as she lifted the heavy roasting pan out of the oven.

‘Smells good,’ she said. ‘We’ll let it rest for a while.’

‘And who’s going to carve?’ he asked, looking worried.

‘You of course,’ she said, then saw his face. ‘We’ll take turns,’ she laughed. ‘Don’t worry, Ralph’s a dab hand at cooking and carving – he’s had to be. Let’s go and have a Christmas drink before I dish up the vegetables and call the boys.’

They left the kitchen together, Eden close behind Janet. Then he turned her round to face him and kissed her gently on the mouth.

She was surprised how moved she was, and clung to him for a moment – as the boys came down the stairs.

‘Glad to see the mistletoe being used,’ David grinned.

‘Did you put that up there – cheeky devil,’ Janet said, flustered and not a little warm, whether from the heat of the kitchen or Eden’s kiss she wasn’t sure.

Surveying the table, and pleased with herself for cooking what was a really good Christmas meal, she was delighted for all their sakes, Eden, Ralph and young David – did the boys miss a father? They hardly ever mentioned him, which sometimes she thought as odd. He rarely contacted them – only birthdays and Christmas, when he remembered. It was too late now. But thinking of Eden's suggestion the other evening, of course she had thought about it. Not living together – she could never sanction that – but well – being an item, as they said today. Even if they didn't share a house together. She liked Eden, more than somewhat and she felt he liked her. Could they . . . would they . . . that the boys approved of him was obvious. They talked football, sports, although she could see Ralph was drawing farther away from home with every year. That was as it should be.

But David and Eden really got on, surprising really, for Eden was not a macho man, in that sense.

They were all flushed with wine, and replete from a good meal, when she brought in the Christmas pudding which she had made herself. A small one, for she knew none of them were that keen and would rather have ice cream, which she used as an alternative with a home-made trifle.

David chose that moment to ask if it would be all right if his friend Tom could come to dinner on the day after Boxing Day and Ralph said he would be going out with his friend. They were going up to London.

'The girlfriend?' Janet asked. She had quite liked her.

'No, Bill Wright, he's at college with me,' Ralph said and Janet breathed again.

No one wanted coffee – they would have tea later and Janet asked them all to carry the dishes into the kitchen. She stacked them. One day she would buy a dishwasher, it was her dearest wish.

By four o'clock it was growing darker, and the television was on.

'It's not bad out, what about a short walk?' she suggested.

'I'm game,' Eden said, getting to his feet.

'Let's walk down through the garden and I'll show you the apple orchard,' Janet said.

Wrapped up in warm coats and scarves, they left the boys to television, while they walked on the dry, crackling leaves, down to the orchard below the back garden. The trees were bare but you could see for miles.

Eden pulled Janet to a stop and took her hand.

'This is as good a spot as any,' he said, bending and kissing her again, and this time Janet didn't want him to stop.

'Oh, Eden—'

'Jan, let's get married,' he said. 'I mean it – what are we waiting for?'

'Eden!'

'Why not?'

'I don't know,' she said slowly, 'I suppose, I'm surprised that's all, after all these years.' And yet it seemed right somehow.

'I'm slow on the uptake,' he said.

She put her arms around his neck.

'Oh, you're not. You're a wonderful man,' she said, and she meant every word of it.

'You mean – you will?'

'Well,' she said slowly. 'We've just had a lovely meal – and lots of wine – ask me again – about ten o'clock.'

'You think I don't mean it, don't you?'

'No,' she said. 'I'm sure you do but ask me again.'

They continued walking, every now and again stopping, their arms around each other.

David got up to draw the curtains and saw them coming back up the drive, arms round each other.

He grinned. I might have a new dad, he thought. I hope so – I like Eden Brook. We've a lot in common – he likes Becks same as me . . .

The household was quiet at one o'clock in the morning, Janet had gone to bed, Eden gone home, the boys still watching television.

She would tell them tomorrow. For Eden had asked her

again and she knew she would. She was so excited she knew she wouldn't sleep.

She was unaware that some hours previously her dear friend Mrs Bancroft had died in her sleep, as little trouble in death as she had been in life.

Chapter Nineteen

For Ruth, as Christmas Day dawned, it seemed an overcast warm kind of day, not at all the snowy white Christmas that the youngsters looked forward to, which older people knew could look wonderful but be treacherous to the traveller.

Up early, as usual, her presents boxed and ready, Ruth made herself a cup of coffee. Her second Christmas without John. Very strange. Last year had been a turmoil, with so much to do, coming to terms with her loss and an oddly unreal situation. This year was different. But it didn't seem right without John.

Soon, though, she would be with her family. She looked around the room at her displayed cards. She still received cards from ex-pupils and from her sons, the boys as she still called them, and one from Charles, her eldest grandson now in Washington, and ex-neighbours, and suddenly she thought of Julie. Julie Stringer, as she now was. No card from Julie – how very out of character – and she felt a sudden apprehension.

She had been unwell, or resting, the woman had said. Was it Norah she had spoken to – the help she had seen on her visit? Resting and not wanting to be disturbed. She wished now she had telephoned in the last couple of days – she could hardly telephone on Christmas Day. She must put Julie out of her mind over Christmas. No good would come of dwelling on that situation.

Later, she stacked the car with gifts and food contributions to the Christmas festivities, nuts and special fruit, boxed chocolates and a special cake from Coppins, the homemade bakery, although she knew it would be no better than the ones Alice made. But every little helped a family for Christmas – it was an expensive time.

Francesca and Alistair had gone to his brother for Christmas and she wondered how they were getting on. The house looked bleak with the blinds drawn and no one there. Lights on this early in Janet's house – she hoped they had a good time, the family deserved it. In the distance, up Notcutts Lane, she could also see all the lights on in Greystones.

Time she got going, in case she met heavy traffic, but there was not much traffic about, and she made the journey easily, coming at last to the fringes of a town, so different from a country area, with its well-kept gardens and immaculate houses. There were lots of Christmas lights on – some people had made a festive display in their front gardens.

But Alice's house was not like that. Immaculate, swept, and yes, by the porch with its two tubs and dwarf conifers, a single bulb surrounded with holly. A Christmas light shone over the door and, as she approached, the sound of the two dogs barking could be heard – always a sign that you had arrived at Alice's house. Gus, a spaniel, a good-natured dog, and Hideous Kinky as Ruth called her, her real name being much more exotic, Tatiana – something like that, Ruth could never remember.

Jamie came out of the computer room (where else?); he was like his father, tall for six, and thin with a cheeky smile.

The kitchen resembled nothing so much as a high-class restaurant, with every conceivable kind of gadget. From its depths Alice emerged, cooking apron over her

Christmas dress, a smudge of flour on her flushed cheeks, and hugged her mother.

'Come and see the dining room, Gran,' the children said, and she followed them. It was indeed splendid. The long table, laid out specially for Christmas with the best dinner service, candles everywhere, soft music from King's College Chapel in the background and delicious smells everywhere of Christmas-Day cooking.

The Christmas tree was a splendid affair. Beautifully decorated by the children – the whole family seemed to have inherited Alice's talent on how to run a home successfully. Nothing was left out.

Her son-in-law returned from seeing his mother who lived some way off, greeted her, and took the two dogs for a walk.

'Now, how about a drink?' Alice said, taking off her apron, 'before we open pressies.' They always opened presents with an accompanying drink before lunch, in the same way that Ruth and John had done when they had a young family.

Alice sat on the floor, and began handing the parcels around. Ruth was very proud of her. I wonder if I did as well when my family were young, she wondered. Not at cooking – that was never my strong point. But there was nothing like a family gathered together for Christmas and she thought, quite naturally of the many Christmases she and John had spent surrounded by their family – it was the best time of your life, did you but know it. Later, when they all disappeared and had homes of their own you realised what a wonderful time it had been. But that was the order of things. What goes around, comes around.

Then Geoff telephoned from Dubai, where the temperature was goodness knows what, and Robert phoned from Washington. They all exchanged greetings and good wishes with promises to see each other soon.

'How about a drink, Mummy?' Alice asked.

Everyone had a drink and was surrounded by coloured paper and boxes and cries of 'Oh, lovely, just what I wanted!' Ruth's eyes glistened. Family – there was nothing like it.

Afterwards, when the paper had been collected and the presents piled up beside each owner, she asked Alice if there was anything to do in the kitchen. The least she could do, she thought, but it was fairly obvious that everything was under control.

Jamie had disappeared back to his games in the computer room.

'Won't see him for the rest of the day,' Anna said, 'Well, except for lunch,' which turned out to be a gourmet's dream, the girls both helping to serve the delicious fresh fruit starter to the roast turkey and bread sauce, the roast vegetables with every kind of dressing and herb. They took their time, not wanting to rush such an excellent meal.

Alice served a sorbet, she was good at that, and then much later, the pudding, which was plum, and lemon tart, and a choice of cold sweets, some of which the girls had helped make.

'They all take after you,' Ruth said. 'It's amazing.'

'Anna has a fine recipe for French dressing – give it to Gran before she goes, Anna.'

'Yes. I will.'

Eventually lunch was over, the girls helped their father to clear away, then went up to their rooms, and Alice and Ruth sat side by side on the sofa.

'You must be tired. Why don't you go up and rest?' Ruth said. 'It was a splendid lunch.'

'Yes, it was good, wasn't it? No, I'm not tired – it's all in a day's work.' Alice said.

Eventually, the conversation got round to Julie.

'So, what news?' Alice asked.

'Well, nothing. I told you. The help, or someone, said she didn't wish to be disturbed.'

'She couldn't have known it was you.'

'I thought it strange. I'm worried about her.'

'Oh, she'll be all right, remember how much her life must have changed. I think it is a pity she married him though.'

Ruth turned bright eyes to her. 'Do you, Alice? I know I do, and I don't know why.'

'We don't like change – we want it to stay the same.'

'Thank you, Gran,' the children chorused.

'I want to come over to see your cottage in the holidays,' Anna said.

'Me, too,' Louisa said.

So amid many thanks, she made her farewells, and started back on the journey to Apple Tree Cottage.

Nevertheless, once out of the road, she felt a tear escape. Concentrate, she told herself. It's coming up a bit misty.

Eden was on the phone early on Boxing Day morning. Janet wasn't asleep – she was too excited to sleep.

'Happy Boxing Day,' he said. 'You haven't changed your mind, have you, Jan?'

She smiled. She hadn't felt so happy for a long time. 'No, have you?'

'Not a chance,' he said. 'Am I going to see you today?'

'I hope so,' she said. 'Come round when you like – lunch time and we'll finish off the turkey.'

'Oh, that will be great,' he said.

When he arrived, he took her in his arms, and she felt at last that she had come home. She was at peace. It seemed inevitable – that she and Eden should come together. Above all was the thought that the boys approved. Ralph said little, but she knew that he thought it was okay. David seemed positively pleased.

David was drinking orange juice from the fridge, Ralph still upstairs in his room.

'I can't understand,' David said to Eden, 'why you

follow Charlton Athletic.'

'Simple. I was born there. Charlton in south-east London. My dad had a tailor's business there and decided to move to the Cotswolds for my mother's health. I've always been a Charlton fan,' said Eden, and somehow David accepted that.

'Still, you like Beckham, don't you?'

'He's the greatest,' Eden said, winking at Janet.

What a Christmas, she thought. Who would have believed it?

When David had gone back upstairs, Eden and Janet took a walk into the garden. It was a warm, muggy day, not at all Christmasy.

'I couldn't be more excited,' Eden said.

She leaned over and kissed him.

'You're sure you think we are doing the right thing?'

'Absolutely,' he said. 'No doubt at all.'

'Where will we live?' Janet asked.

'Up to you,' he said. 'I don't care as long as we are together.'

'Come and live at Plum Tree Cottage,' she said. 'It can't be nice living over a shop all these years.'

'No, it isn't,' he said. 'But I'm used to it, I've always done it.'

'But wouldn't you like—'

'Yes, of course, if you are agreeable, and Janet, let's go in and tell the boys that we are going to be married, shall we?'

They clung together in the misty, fruit-scented garden.

What a future lay in front of her, Janet thought. It was up to her to deserve it. Tomorrow she would go along to Greystones and tell Mrs Bancroft the news. She will be pleased.

She watched Eden raking leaves in the garden. Oh, it was nice to have a man around the house again. She sighed. Who would have thought it this time last week?

She would go tomorrow to Greystones to see Mrs

Bancroft. It would seem odd with Edith Willis away in Scotland and Mrs Bligh somewhere in her swish hotel. Wouldn't she be surprised at her news? She hoped Mrs Bancroft had not been too lonely.

Mrs Woolsbridge answered the door to her knock, looking even more serious than usual. 'Come in, Janet,' she said.

Janet knew by her face that there was something wrong.

'What is it?' she asked, an awful fear spreading through her.

'Come through,' Mrs Woolsbridge said, and led Janet through to her private domain. 'Sit down, my dear.'

Warm words from Mrs Woolsbridge.

'I am sorry to tell you that Mrs Bancroft died – on Christmas Eve. Peacefully, probably from a heart attack. She wouldn't have suffered.'

She would never see her again. Part of her life had gone. She couldn't believe it.

'Of course, it has been a little quiet with the other two away but I can assure you everything was done. She had already died when I went up to see how she was. There will have to be a post-mortem, of course, and the funeral will probably take place next week but it will be a private family affair. Of course, it was a shock but the best way to go ...'

Janet was stunned. After that wonderful Christmas – and now this. Poor Mrs Bancroft, and no one there to help her – that's all she could think of.

'Could I—'

Mrs Woolsbridge shook her head, but quite kindly. 'No, my dear. Better not. In any case,' she stopped and looked at Janet. 'I know you will miss her – we all will, but try to look on the bright side. She was not very happy and probably felt she had come to the end of the road.'

How would you know, thought Janet angrily, but she

said nothing. Handkerchief pressed to her mouth, she slowly left the room, but turned at the front door.

'Thank you, Mrs Woolsbridge.'

Mrs Woolsbridge inclined her head.

Chapter Twenty

As Christmas came and went, Ruth became more and more worried about Julie's state of health.

Janet had been in to see her and told her the sad news of Mrs Bancroft's death. She seemed quite cut up about it. Edith Willis was still away in Scotland, so things were not as normal in the nursing home.

Ruth telephoned Julie's old flat, with no result; then on the third day she rang the residence in Park Lane.

'Who is this speaking?' she was asked.

'Ruth Durling, Mrs Durling, an old friend of Mrs Stringer,' she replied. 'I have been trying to get through to her since before Christmas. Is she away?'

'No, she is here, but unfortunately she is unwell, and is unable to come to the telephone.'

'Could I speak to her husband, Mr Stringer?' Ruth asked.

'No, I am afraid that is not possible,' the voice replied.

'To whom am I speaking?' Ruth asked at length.

'Nurse Logan,' the voice said.

'Are you nurse to Mrs or Mr Stringer?'

'I am afraid I cannot answer any more questions. I will tell Mrs Stringer that you called.'

So *she* could talk to Julie. That much was possible. She was quite mystified.

The next day she telephoned again and received the same message. But she persisted.

'I am most anxious to talk to Mrs Stringer – is that possible? I am a very old friend.'

'No, she is quite ill, and I am afraid is not allowed telephone calls. I will tell her you called.'

'What is wrong with her?'

'I am afraid I cannot answer your questions – only the doctor can do that.'

'May I have a word with him – will you give me his telephone number?' but she was cut short.

'No, I am afraid I cannot do that—'

'Can you put me through to Mr Stringer?'

'No, I am sorry—'

That night she couldn't sleep – imagining all sorts of things. It was a mystery – if Julie was ill, say with flu or pneumonia, anything, they could have told her. She was not in hospital.

The next day she decided. She would go up to town to see her. It was the only way. It was not the best day for travelling. Frosty roads, there had been a severe frost overnight, the fields were white, and the paths slippery so she decided to take a taxi to the station just in case things got worse during the day and she could not drive home.

Sitting back in the train, she was glad she had done this. Perhaps she was over-reacting but at least she would find out for herself.

Surprisingly the streets were crowded with shoppers, for the January sales were on. They had started in December and she had forgotten about that. No wonder the trains had been packed.

A taxi took her to Park Lane, and the commissionaire on the door asked her business. When she said she was a friend of Mrs Stringer who was ill and she was visiting her, he allowed her in. What a change from the last time she had been here!

She rang the bell, and knocked on the door, and a nurse in uniform opened the door. She smiled, pleasantly.

'I am Mrs Durling, a friend of Mrs Stringer. Could I see her for a moment or two?'

'I am sorry, Mrs Stringer is not allowed visitors.'

'I am a close friend of hers, and I have been telephoning every day. I have come a long way, and I wish to see her.'

She looked and sounded adamant.

She saw Norah pass through the hall and glance in her direction, looking worried, and then she heard Bertie Stringer's voice, grumbling from way off.

Norah returned and spoke to the nurse softly.

'Very well, you may come in, but for a moment, mind.'

With a huge feeling of relief, Ruth stepped inside. Lord, how she hated this place. The nurse led her through the enormous hall and, glancing to her left, she could see Bertie Stringer in his wheelchair with his back to her, and another uniformed nurse at his side. They seemed miles away in this huge apartment.

The first nurse led her through to another bedroom, and Ruth recognised it as one of the spare bedrooms. She tapped on the door but without waiting for an answer went in and whispered something to the person lying on the bed.

Ruth followed her.

She hardly recognised Julie, lying there still, a yellowy pallor on her face. She held out a limp hand towards Ruth, who clasped it. She didn't know this Julie, with her dark hair spread over the pillows, the grey in it, the sunken eyes which held a glow of recognition.

'You came.' Her voice was a whisper.

Near to tears, Ruth clasped her hand. 'Julie, dear, I was so worried about you.'

'Christmas,' Julie whispered.

'Yes, I wanted to come before.'

Not to start this now, to explain her worries – this woman was dying, there was no doubt of that. How could it have happened? But this was no time for questions like that.

'I brought you some flowers.' And she put them on the

bedside table – but they were unimportant.

She gripped Julie's hand tightly, and the large diamond cut into her hand.

Julie gave a weak smile. 'Margaret's,' she said.

Ruth was near to tears. There seemed nothing to say – how did you – where – why?

It was too late for that. Julie was dying.

'Are you well?' Julie whispered.

Ruth nodded. 'But we must get you well soon – I'll come and have lunch with you,' she said through her tears, and was rewarded with a glimmer of humour in the dark eyes which seemed to her to be even now fading away into the distance.

Oh, I can't bear it, thought Ruth and took her other hand. 'You are to get well,' she said, 'and come and stay with me, remember?'

Such thoughts were far away.

Nurse Logan stood at her side.

'I'm afraid you will have to go now, Mrs Durling,' she said, and whispered, 'she is very weak.'

Ruth could see that. She didn't want to stay now. She knew how near the end was.

She bent down and kissed Julie gently. 'Goodbye darling,' she said and felt a faint pressure from Julie's hand.

Then she left and didn't look back. She couldn't bear to.

Outside, she took a grip on herself. 'What is wrong with her?' she said severely to Nurse Logan.

'I cannot answer that. You will have to ask her doctor.'

It was all too late. She glanced along the huge corridor where she could see the wheelchair and in it the old man, who didn't even give her the courtesy of looking round.

The nurse showed her the door, and the commissionaire touched his cap.

She took a deep breath. Oh, it was good to get out of there.

She hailed a taxi. As the thoughts wheeled round in her head and would not go away, she caught the train back to Little Astons almost without realising what she was doing. She sat in the train, stiffly, as if in a dream, only stirring when she came to the station before her own, slightly startled to see the white fields around her and only then, as she reached her station, did she almost fall out of the carriage, her sadness and shock overwhelming her. Blindly she rushed – full tilt into a tall man who was obviously waiting to get on the train.

He held her, steadied her. 'Mrs Durling, Ruth,' and caught her and held her.

He held her closely for some time, his arms around her, until she looked up and with yet another shock saw that it was Martin Amesbury. She eased herself out of his arms.

Breathlessly, she dabbed at her face, at the tears that had drenched it – and still he held her arm.

The train started up and he let it go.

'Come,' he said. 'My car is at the station car park. Did you leave yours there?'

She shook her head, still in a state of shock.

'Then I'll drive you home.'

Gratefully, she sank into the seat beside him, aware that he was driving carefully over the roads, wet now with the continual traffic. He pulled up outside Apple Tree Cottage and automatically she got out the keys and gave them to him.

He unlocked the door, showed her in and led her to the big easy chair. Then he went into the kitchen and put on a kettle.

'Tea?' he said, 'or something stronger?'

'Tea, first,' she said and tried to smile.

When it was all ready, he brought it on a tray and pouring a cup handed it to her.

He sat down opposite her. 'Do you feel like telling me about it?'

Yes, she thought, I must talk about it. She felt she wanted to talk to someone, and why not this man, who had been so kind.

She gave him a weepy smile. 'You seem very much at home here,' she said.

'I lived here quite a bit, with my grandparents, my mother's parents,' he said. 'As a child, it was my second home.'

Oh, that explained it.

'And was it your grandfather who laid out the garden?'

'Yes,' he said. 'It was. But tell me what happened today.'

The tea was hot and comforting and she sank back in the armchair still unable to believe that she had been to London and back and seen Julie and that she was dying. He said nothing except to ask if she would like the fire turned on – it was a gas fire and it was comforting, and she said she did. He seemed to have all the time in the world, and sat on the sofa prepared, it seemed, to wait until she wanted to talk.

'You are very kind,' she said presently. 'I am so sorry. I had had such a shock but – you were about to catch the train, weren't you?'

He smiled. 'No problem. It wasn't important. I was just going into Cheltenham but I can go tomorrow. Tell me what happened.'

And she began to talk with meeting Julie – how they met, their spasmodic friendship, which had grown over the years. It all poured out as he listened. Julie's meeting with Albert – Bertie Stringer – his proposal, his suggestion about the money, the Park Lane flat and at times he frowned and looked puzzled.

It wasn't until she came to the part where she had become worried since Julie's marriage, when she said she had made up her mind to visit her and what she found when she went to the flat in Park Lane that she saw his eyes widen.

He went over to her. 'Ruth, what a shock. Here, let me get you a drink. Do you drink whisky?'

'Not as a rule,' she said.

'But it's good for you – a pick-me-up,' he said. 'May I?'

And she watched as he got two glasses out of the cabinet and poured them each a glass of whisky from the decanter on the sideboard.

'Drink this,' he said and she sipped it, hating the taste – and memories of John came flooding back. She associated the drink with him although he only ever had one when he came home in the evening while she had wine. It was heart-warming though, and seemed to stabilise her.

He sat back. 'Quite a story,' he said. 'And I can understand how you feel. But often the lives of others are almost unbelievable, aren't they?'

'I feel all this is a dream.' This too, she wanted to add.

'And you are sure she is dying?' he said.

'Oh, I am sure,' she said.

'Very sad,' he said, 'and a shock for you.'

'I don't know how to tell my daughter. She was fond of her too. Aunt Julie, as she called her.'

'You have a daughter?' he asked.

'Yes, Alice,' she said.

'I too, have a daughter,' he said, 'Sarah. She is married and lives in South Africa.'

She smiled back at him. 'You have been very kind,' she said. 'I was quite beside myself.'

'These things come as a shock,' he said. 'I suggest you take it easy – perhaps have a rest this afternoon.'

'I can't think,' she worried, 'what was wrong with her?'

'You may never know,' he said. 'Try to accept it – there is nothing you can do.'

'You are a practical man,' she said.

'I've had to be. Well, I must go now,' he said, picking up his driving gloves.

'You have been very kind. I am most grateful – listening to me ...'

'You were very upset,' he said. 'Understandably.'

She didn't add, I didn't imagine you would be like this.

He took her hand briefly. 'I'll go now and I will give you a ring tomorrow to see how you are.'

The door closed behind him. She missed him already. A steady influence – a man around the house.

She telephoned the next day, and with no surprise learned that Julie had died that night. She asked to speak to Norah.

Norah came on and in a low voice explained that the funeral would be at Golders Green the following Wednesday.

'I should go if you want to,' Norah whispered. 'It's at two forty-five,' and put down the phone.

And I will, Ruth said to herself. It's called paying respects . . .

When Martin rang that evening to enquire how she was, she told him that Julie had died. He sympathised with her, and asked if she was all right.

'Yes, thank you,' she answered. 'And I shall go to the funeral.'

'Is that wise?'

'I want to go,' she said, and braced herself to ring Alice, waiting until she was home in the evening.

'Alice,' she said. 'All well with you?'

'You just caught me – just came in the door. Everything all right?'

'Well, sad news, Julie—'

There was a pause. 'You don't mean—'

'Julie died.' she heard Alice's gasp.

'Julie died? How could she die? She wasn't ill, was she?'

'Apparently she was. I went up to see her – had to force my way there, actually – but I won't go into that now, I know I am jolly glad I did. I saw her, and she was very ill.'

'But what was wrong with her?'

'I don't know, and the nurse wouldn't tell me.'

'You can always ask to see the death certificate.'

'Oh, I wouldn't do that – after all, she is no relation, but a dear friend – or was,' and she could hear Alice quietly sniffing in the background.

'Oh, Mummy! How awful! She was no age.'

'No, that's right. Well, I am going to the funeral.'

'You're not!'

'I am, I want to go – I feel somehow it's the least I can do.'

'Where is it?'

'Golders Green.'

'You're not going all the way up there, oh, Mummy!'

'I am, it's no distance, really.'

'I can't come with you, I'm working.'

'And no reason why you should. Don't worry – I'll tell you all about it when I get back sometime.'

'Well, take care,' and sniffing, Alice put down the phone.

Ruth allowed several hours in which to make the journey to Paddington then change for the tube to Golders Green where she bought a posy of red roses.

She had quite a long wait, for the crematorium was busy and the services were in strict rotation.

Once inside the little chapel, way ahead she could see a wheelchair in the front with two uniformed nurses. Behind, the only mourner in sight, was Norah.

At the back of the chapel sat about twenty women. All very well dressed, mostly in black, elegant, upright, a most impressive little crowd. Ruth took her place behind them.

The service was short, the shortest Ruth ever remembered, the organ piped Handel, and it was over.

Ruth was one of the first outside, feeling as strange as she had ever felt in her life. She was joined by the women who looked at her, then spoke. 'Were you a client of Julie Pinkerton?'

She noticed they didn't give her married name. 'Yes.'

'We are,' they all said and stood to one side, as a nurse came out pushing the old man in the wheelchair, who glanced neither to the right nor the left, but was put into a black Rolls-Royce without a word.

They looked after him. 'Poor Julie,' one of them said.

'Are you all clients?' Ruth asked.

'Indeed we are – or ex-clients.'

One of them, an elegant middle-aged woman spoke. 'Why don't we all go for coffee to the nearest hotel, then we'll drink to Julie's health in some other place?'

'Yes, let's,' said Ruth and followed them.

'Oh, she was darling.'

'I loved her to bits.'

'Why do you think – I didn't even know she was ill.'

Then out of the corner of her eye she saw Norah, who seemed at a loss. 'Norah,' she said.

Norah dabbed her eyes. 'She was a lovely lady,' she said.

'Norah, what did she die of – I mean what was her illness?'

Norah put her hand over her mouth. 'I think,' and she stumbled over the words. 'Cirrhosis – of the liver?'

Ruth was shocked. 'Oh!' and joined the others.

All the way home in the train she wondered. Wasn't it to do with drinking? Had Julie drunk that much? Had she always been a drinker? It was difficult to come to terms with that but she had to die with something – and that awful old man . . .

Arriving home, she found Martin Amesbury's car in the drive. He was sitting in it – waiting for her.

She smiled, her first of the day. 'Oh, how nice. How long have you been waiting?'

'Not long. I worked out the trains and I've got a heater on, so I'm not cold.'

'Oh, come inside,' she said warmly. 'Let's have a

drink.' And then she stopped short.
'Yes, let's have a drink,' she said. 'Warm us up.'
So pleased she was to see him.

Chapter Twenty-One

On a bleak, cold morning in January Janet made her way to the little church.

St Luke's was a church she had known well in the days of her childhood. Morning and evening service, and Sunday school in the afternoon in the room adjoining, but they had all attended the services. Been made to, but they had been glad to see their friends, meet up and have fun after the service, for Sundays were always so bleak. No shops open – adults sitting around reading the newspapers, the fathers having a snooze after Sunday lunch.

Inside the church the organ was playing softly, but there were not many people there. She sat at the back, not wishing to intrude, and saw Mrs Woolsbridge there, and a tall middle-aged man with a younger man, probably Mrs Bancroft's grandson. Then in came the daughter, well wrapped up in a tweed coat and scarf, and a furry hat, moving swiftly and looking businesslike.

She still couldn't believe it. It had happened so swiftly – poor Mrs Bancroft. She wouldn't stay for the interment – after all, she was not part of the family but just wished to pay her respects. The eulogy was read – what did they know of her dear Mrs Bancroft or how much she would miss her? Quietly, she went outside and walked home.

It was a week later that the letter came, from Mr Chadwick, the local solicitor.

14, King's Row
Little Astons
Glos.

Dear Mrs Foster
The late Mrs Violet Bancroft
It is with very great regret that I write to inform you of the death of Mrs Bancroft and to inform you that under the terms of her Will she has left you a small oil painting. You may see this whenever you wish but it will be about eight to ten weeks before we will be able to obtain a Grant of Probate and release any legacies but I will keep you informed of the developments.
Yours sincerely
Norman Chadwick

Janet stifled a gasp. A painting – left to her – it must be the little picture which had hung on Mrs Bancroft's wall – the painting of Amsterdam by the Dutchman. How lovely, but what would Mrs Bancroft's family say? Perhaps it was valuable, in which case she could hardly accept it.

Now she was worried. Oh, Mrs Bancroft shouldn't have done that! She must tell Eden about it – and didn't know whether to be pleased or upset.

'Well!' Eden said when she told him. 'That's great. How kind of her but then I bet you were good to her. You've a kind heart, Janet.'

'But there was no need to give me that – it might be valuable. I mean, I am not family.'

'What makes you think it might be valuable?'

'I don't know, it looks as if it might be.'

'Well,' he said. 'She wanted you to have it. She wanted to show her gratitude to you.'

'Suppose it's worth a lot of money.' Janet was worried.

'So much the better,' Eden said. 'After all, you need all the money you can get if you want to buy the salon.'

'Typical man!' she said punching him lightly. 'I'm

worried that the family will disapprove – her daughter is a bit of a so and so.'

'Let's worry about that when we come to it,' he said, practically.

The whole village was delighted with the news that Eden Brook and Janet Foster were to marry. Many of the older inhabitants had thought they were made for each other from the beginning – they were a popular couple.

Ruth was delighted. She had become fond of Janet – such a warm-hearted woman and, from the little she had seen of Eden Brook, they seemed ideally suited.

She tried to allay Janet's fears about the opposition she might get from the family. 'You mustn't worry about that. It was Mrs Bancroft's personal wish and there is nothing they can do about that. And imagine, Janet, if it is valuable, it might be useful when it comes to buying the salon.'

Janet sounded shocked. 'Oh, I shouldn't like to do that. It is a personal gift from her to me, it's awful to think of selling it.'

'But I am sure that's why she has given it to you. She would want you to get the most out of it. If selling it gives you what you want, she would be pleased.'

'Anyway,' Janet said. 'I'm not going to worry about the value, the picture itself is lovely. You would like it. I couldn't think of selling it, it would be wrong.'

'Well,' Ruth said mildly, 'you might think differently if you find out it's worth a lot of money and I am sure you could do with it – most of us could – but you particularly with the salon sale coming up.'

'It's like a wedding present, really,' Janet said slowly. 'I feel sorry she never knew Eden and I were going to be married.'

'Perhaps she had an inkling,' Ruth said. 'You just never know and perhaps that's what she had in mind.'

So, on a very cold February morning, Janet and Eden were married by special dispensation in the little church.

Everyone was there who could be, and a reception was held in Janet's home. Ralph came down from university for the day, and David stayed home from school. The two boys seemed delighted with their new father, for Eden was to move into the cottage after the wedding.

It was a very happy little gathering which crowded into Janet's small sitting room. Even Fran and Alistair were there, and lots of neighbours, and Miss Willis and Nell Bligh, who rose splendidly to the occasion by daring to wear her mink coat over her violet satin dress. And, when Martin arrived later, Ruth surprised herself by being pleased to see him.

The champagne flowed and the wedding cake was cut amid much hilarity, after which Martin took Ruth to one side.

'Just as we are getting on so well,' he said ruefully. 'I am going away for a week.' Ruth found herself feeling very disappointed.

'My daughter in South Africa, I've just had a telephone call. She has just had a baby son, so I'm off tomorrow to visit her. My first grandchild. Just for a week,' he said almost apologetically.

'Congratulations,' Ruth said. 'A grandson, that's wonderful news. Oh, yes you must go.'

He smiled down at her. 'I shall miss you,' he said and turned away to greet Janet.

Had he really said that? wondered Ruth. She sat down next to Alistair, to have a chat with him. How much his life must have altered. 'Well, this is the year you move into your new bungalow,' she smiled. 'Are you looking forward to it?'

'Yes, it's going to be great. We drove over yesterday to see it, it's a bit bleak at the moment, they've finished the building – so now it's a question of fitting up the interior.'

'I've just had a thought, are you free tomorrow evening?'

'Yes, I think so.'

'Come and have dinner with me – you and Fran – I'd like

that, although I don't know that I can find a fourth. Martin is off tomorrow to South Africa – did he tell you?'

'Yes, he has a new grandson, well, his first – so he's very excited.'

Ruth thought she would look forward to planning a meal. She was quite out of touch – time she got some practice.

Before all the guests left, Martin came over to her to say goodbye. 'I'll see you when I get back,' he said. 'Perhaps we'll go out somewhere to celebrate my new status.' His eyes twinkled. He does have a sense of humour, Ruth decided, and found herself defending him.

There was to be no honeymoon for Janet and Eden, and after the guests had gone, Eden helped her clear away the glasses and dishes.

'First thing,' he said, 'a dishwasher. A family needs one.'

She did believe he was going to enjoy his new role as stepfather.

She looked down at her ring. Her left hand had been bare since she left Jack. At the wide plain band, and the diamond ring which she and Eden had chosen together. She held it out, so that it shone in the electric light.

'Are you pleased, Jan?' Eden asked. 'Are you happy?'

She put her arms round him and hugged him tightly. 'More than I ever thought I could be,' she said, and knew it to be true.

Before he had left to go back to university, Ralph had hugged her – a very unusual thing – he had never been very demonstrative. It had taken her by surprise and brought tears to her eyes. No doubt then, of his approval.

'Be happy, Mum,' he said, and he was gone.

David had gone round to stay the night with his school-friend but he too had kissed her warmly when he said goodnight.

'You be all right, Mum?' he asked when he left.

Janet threw a swift glance at Eden who was looking at her.

'Oh, I'm sure I will. Now, mind how you go, see you tomorrow.

'Night, Eden,' he said.

The next evening Fran and Alistair came to dinner, Alistair leaning heavily on his stick. It was a bitterly cold night, and Ruth had cooked what she knew she did best: a warming meal, roast beef and Yorkshires, preceded by carrot and coriander soup and, to end with, apple pie and cheese.

'Your daughter surely gets her cooking skills from you,' Fran observed.

'No, I'd like to think so, but not so. She is a born cook, while my efforts are a hit-and-miss affair and I usually cook what I do best when I entertain. Now, sit back and relax and we'll have coffee.'

They talked of the wedding the previous day and of how everyone had wished Jan and Eden to be married. 'They were a match from the start when they were in their teens,' Fran observed. 'If it hadn't been for that Fenella, who certainly put the cat among the pigeons, and her ghastly mother. But you'd have to be hard to dismiss Fenella,' she said. 'She was something. That rare creature – beauty and brains and a lot of charm thrown in.'

She raised the remains of her wine glass. 'Anyway, here's to Jan and Eden, together at long last.'

They sat talking for some time, eating chocolate mints while Alistair had a glass of brandy.

'So, Martin is off to South Africa,' Alistair mused. 'I'm delighted for him – he is very fond of his daughter. I bet she doesn't go – Stella—'

'Not her. They've never been very close,' Fran said. 'What do you think of him?' she asked suddenly.

And Ruth found herself flushing to the roots of her hair.

'Me? Well, I've only met him once or twice but he seems very nice,' she said.

But her blush had not gone unnoticed by Fran. 'You must both come to dinner when he gets back,' she said casually.

'Yes, thank you,' Ruth said.

Tucking herself down in the warm bed in Apple Tree Cottage she thought that, on reflection, she had made a wise move to Little Astons. She had made some good friends and forged a new life for herself. She hoped this year would be as good as last.

February – and she had moved in May last year. How swiftly the time went. You had to live life to the full, if you were able. How soon a man was cut down in his prime, like Alistair. And Julie – but she wouldn't think about that now. Think of Robert coming to visit, and possibly Charles one day, and the other grandchildren, and Martin, on his way to South Africa . . .

'So, what have you been up to?' Alice asked.

'Um, well, we've had a wedding – Janet and Eden Brook. He's the tailor in the village. Janet lives in Notcutts Lane.'

'Oh, that's nice. Divorced, wasn't she?'

'Yes, has two boys . . . and I had two neighbours to dinner last night.'

'Oh, well done – what did you give them?'

'Oh, the usual, soup, roast beef—'

'Bit boring. You should try some new recipes.'

'How are the children?'

'They're fine. By the way, the grandfather clock's stopped. Do you think that man in Little Astons would look at it?'

'I shouldn't think so, he's not a clock man but I could find one for you.'

'Don't worry, it probably didn't like the move. Take care, see you soon.'

Chapter Twenty-Two

A few days after his return from South Africa, Martin called at Apple tree Cottage. The first thing Ruth saw was a huge bouquet of lilies. She never ceased to wonder at the proliferation of these exotic blooms in the dead of winter. As a child, they had never seen flowers like this as this time of year – only chrysanthemums, then daffodils, harbingers of spring . . .

He smiled broadly at her and she felt, not for the first time, how much she had missed him. There was some kind of bond between them she had realised when he was away, although she had been very antagonistic towards him at their first meetings. He had aroused strong feelings in her; she had even been angry but she recognised it for what it was – that he had made an impression on her – not to be thrown off lightly.

Now, she saw him in quite a different light. 'Come in, Martin, lovely to see you,' and she led the way into the kitchen and placed the flowers in water in the sink. 'Thank you,' she said.

'Ah,' he said taking off his gloves and coat and rubbing his hands. 'Nice and warm. I can tell you, it is bitter here after South Africa.'

'I imagine,' she said. 'What would you like – coffee?'

'That would be fine.'

'And you can tell me all about the trip – how exciting!'

'It was.'

'And the baby?'

'Oh, wonderful, he weighed almost eight pounds and looks like his father, Kirk. Lots of dark hair - Sarah is fair.'

'He might lose that - they often do when they have a lot of hair.'

'I am so pleased I went, Ruth. I toyed with the idea for a long time. South Africa is not one of my favourite places but it has a lot going for it - the sun, the warmth, and the well, the desire to see young Joel.'

'Is that his name?' Ruth asked. 'Excuse me, I'll get the coffee.'

She came back with the tray of steaming coffee, and Martin again surveyed the cottage.

'You know, you've done wonders with this place. My old grandparents wouldn't recognise it.'

'Still, it was special then, wasn't it?'

'Yes, I loved it - loved staying here.' He took his coffee from her.

'So go on, tell me more about your daughter - is she well? A normal birth - no problems?'

'No, absolutely fine and, as I say, young Joel is super.'

He sat looking into the fire for a moment. 'I wish his grandmother would go and visit Sarah but, well, she is not going to. I don't think Sarah minds as much as I do.'

How much was he going to tell her, Ruth wondered, knowing she would be embarrassed. She didn't want to think of another woman in Martin's life - but his wife . . . They must have been married a long time.

He put down his coffee cup. 'She left me - Stella - my wife. I expect you heard it round the village. Nothing's sacred.'

'Yes, I did hear,' Ruth said quietly. 'But please don't tell me about it if you'd rather not. You don't have to explain anything to me.'

'I want to,' he said.

'It was about the time you arrived,' he said. 'She had always threatened to leave me but I think the business held her back. She loves the antiques world and she is a very good businesswoman – all aspects of it. So we had that in common. That's how we met – at an auction.'

He looked at her. 'One day – she just left. Didn't say anything, went to an auction in Bath, stayed overnight – we often did if it was a big auction, then phoned the next morning to say she wasn't coming back ... and that was that.'

What a cruel thing to do, Ruth thought – but then she had no idea of the real truth behind it and was not sure she wanted to know.

'I expect you are thinking – there's more to it than that, and I daresay there is, apart from the business. We had not a lot in common. We were as different as chalk from cheese but there are many happy marriages where that works.'

She wanted to ask him: was Stella attractive to men, did she like men, was she bored, but it was nothing to do with her.

'I think she found me boring,' he admitted. 'After all, the business is my life, while she was interested in all sorts of things. She didn't get on with Sarah – Sarah has always been a daddy's girl and that didn't please her. That's just the way it was. Anyway, I thought I'd tell you.'

'That can't be easy,' Ruth said. 'And I am sorry – I always hate to hear of broken marriages. Without wishing to brag, after all, it's the luck of the draw, isn't it – I had a happy marriage. At least, I say that and I believe John thought so. We were both busy, working all day – except when I had the children – I am not sure it was terribly exciting but then I hadn't expected it to be. We were compatible, that's the word, and you and your wife, obviously were not. Luck of the draw, as I say ...'

She looked up at him, and wondered how fond he had been of his wife. Did he miss her? Was he devastated? It had certainly put him in a rotten mood at the time, but then

– there must always be a sense of failure with a broken marriage, whoever was at fault.

She decided to change the subject. 'I had Fran and Alistair to dinner the night you left – they are a great couple.'

He smiled. 'Yes, they are, Fran is a lot more vulnerable than she appears. Alistair's illness has devastated her – it was the last thing she expected.'

'Then she hides it very well. It's nice having them as neighbours. I shall miss them when they move on.'

He looked across to where the clock had stood. 'Do you miss the clock?' he asked.

'Not really, glad of the space,' she smiled. 'My daughter's thrilled to bits, oh, except that it has stopped going.'

'I can put her in touch with a good man,' he said, 'if she needs one, that is.'

There was gleam of amusement in his eye. 'We didn't get off to a very good start, did we?'

'No, I thought you were appallingly rude!' Ruth said.

'God, did you? Was I that bad?'

'Yes, you were, airing your knowledge – very superior, I thought – rude sod!'

He laughed out loud. 'Did you, did you really?' Then he sobered up. 'Well, I was shattered. The last thing I wanted to know about was longcase clocks and you were a bit toffee-nosed about your Regency clock.'

'I was? Well, I thought it was – it had belonged to John – he thought the world of it.'

'I'm sorry – I was a bit brutal.'

'No, you were an antiques dealer,' she said and their eyes met.

'Do you think we can become friends?'

'I hoped we were,' she said.

'You no longer think I am – superior?'

'Well, a bit, but it's your manner,' and she laughed. 'Seriously, I am glad of your company. I miss my husband, I make no secret of it.'

'In other words – a man around the house ... Will anyone do?'

'Oh, no,' she said, shocked. 'He has to be special.'

He leaned over and took her hand. 'I am a little old-fashioned, I know, can't help that. Can we try to make a go of it? How about coming to dinner with me, Friday night?'

'I should like that ...'

The time passed as they sat talking and when it was time for him to leave Ruth was genuinely sorry to see him go.

February passed into March, and April was just round the corner when Janet received notification from Mrs Bancroft's solicitor that she could claim her inheritance.

Both she and Eden went to collect the painting and Janet had a moment's pang when it was unwrapped to think that the last time she had seen it was on the wall over Mrs Bancroft's bed.

'Oh, it's beautiful!' she said, and Eden was very impressed, but he was more practical.

'Quite valuable, isn't it?' he asked Mr Chadwick.

'Yes. I imagine, so, Mr Brook. You certainly will have to have it valued for insurance purposes.'

'You think it might be—?'

Mr Chadwick smiled drily. 'Possibly,' he said, and carrying the wrapped picture carefully, Eden and Janet made their way home.

Once home, they placed it on the sofa, and sat looking at it.

'I shall always see Mrs Bancroft whenever I look at it,' Janet said her eyes full of tears.

'Well, it has a special meaning for you. To me, it's a great picture – Ludolf Bakhuyzen – I've never heard of him. It's obviously Dutch. Why don't we get Martin to look at it when he's passing?'

'Good idea,' Janet said. 'Now where are we going to hang it?'

'In a special place. The hall is not large enough to show

it off. Why don't we move these two pictures and hang this in its place. I don't want to interfere—'

'Good idea,' Janet said, and they set to work to hang it.

It looked even better on the larger wall. The pale blue sky, a few white clouds and the boats with their red and white sails.

'Oh, it's beautiful,' cried Janet. 'I love it – I could sit and stare at it for hours and see something fresh.'

He put his arm round her shoulders then kissed her swiftly.

'You deserve it,' he said.

A few days later, Martin Amesbury called.

'I heard you wanted to see me,' he said to Janet when she opened the door.

'Yes, about the painting that Mrs Bancroft left me. I didn't want to carry it into the village.'

'No, of course not, it's not a problem. I was passing.'

'My word! Is this it?' He stood and stared, then took out his glasses and put them on.

'I say, Janet, that's great. Looks like a little masterpiece to me. Now, don't get carried away – I'm not into Dutch paintings, but I have a friend who is.'

He stared at it through his glasses, then went over and examined the back. 'Beautiful,' he said. 'I wouldn't mind having that myself!'

'Really, Martin?'

Janet was so pleased, she couldn't wait to tell Eden.

'When are you in, if he should call? He sometimes calls on me Friday, or Saturday?'

'You just tell me when and I'll work round it,' Janet said.

'You don't want a proper valuation, do you? He'll charge for that.'

'No, just to tell us what it is, and if it has any value. I don't want to underestimate it, hanging there in this little cottage but I do love it.'

'So do I,' Martin said.

On Saturday morning, Jules Mettier, London art dealer, called to see Janet and the picture.

'How long has it been hanging there?' was the first thing he asked.

'A week,' Janet said. 'Why?'

'Not the best place for it,' he said, then went up to it, took it down, viewed it through several glasses, turned it over, looked at the back and hung it back again.

'Well, my dear,' he said. 'It looks like a genuine Bakhuyzen. He was the principal marine painter of the Netherlands after the departure of the van de Veldes for England in 1672. He painted for monarchs all over Europe and is said to have given Peter the Great drawing lessons.'

Janet gasped. 'Do you mean it's that old?'

'I think so. I would have to take it away to make a thorough check but, as far as I can see, it is genuine. If you look closely, you can see where it is signed. He made a priority of painting scenes like this of Amsterdam and her trade. Be interesting to know where this came from,' he said, and could scarcely take his eyes off it.

'May I ask how long you have had it. Do you know where it came from?'

'It was left to me,' Janet said. 'In an old lady's will.'

The man whistled. 'Indeed. If you wish me to go further with my investigation I will do so.'

'I will have a word with my husband,' Janet said. How odd the word sounded to her after all these years. 'I will tell him what you have said, and we will discuss it.'

'Yes, I don't advise you to keep it there. Why, you can even see it through the window,' he smiled.

'Thank you,' Janet said, and waited for Eden to come home.

In the meantime, the painting lay under the bed, wrapped in a sheet.

A week later, Martin collected it and took it up to

London for valuation. Janet was slightly relieved when it had gone, but she missed it.

'Well, Janet,' he said when he returned. 'You've been left quite a legacy. They estimate a quarter of a million, or thereabouts – say £220, £250,000 on a good day. It has certainly been authenticated although you have no idea of the provenance.'

'What's that?' Janet asked.

'It's history.'

'Well, I do know that Mrs Bancroft's husband bought it – he was of Dutch extraction she told me – and it was one of the first paintings he bought – early in their marriage, I think, but that's all I know.'

'Well, that's something, but you must insure it, that's certain, then what you will do with it is your business.'

'Oh, it's a bit of a worry.'

'You don't have to sell it, Jan,' Eden said. 'We'll raise a bank loan for the salon – we've got ways of doing that – both of us, jointly. I am going to see you get that shop and the picture will be your insurance against bad times – if any. It's not bad to have a nice figure behind you – a sort of cushion.'

She went over and kissed him. 'We'll see,' she said. 'But you think I'll get the salon?'

'I'm sure you will,' Eden said. 'Because you're worth it.' And they laughed together.

A few days before Fran and Alistair moved to their bungalow, Ruth decided to pre-empt Fran's invitation to her and asked them to dinner, together with Martin.

They saw a lot of each other now and Ruth, with a touch of mischief, decided to ask Alice and her husband Jim.

'Dinner?' Alice said. 'What's it in aid of?'

'Well, mainly the people next door who are leaving and I would like you to meet Martin.'

'Martin? Martin who?'

'Martin Amesbury, a friend of mine.'

There was a silence.
'What are you giving them?'
'I haven't worked it out yet.'
'Shall I bring the dessert?'
'No thanks, I can manage.'
'Seven, then, take care.'

The table was laid, and the cutlery in place, and the dinner nicely cooking in the oven, and the two desserts reposing in the fridge. Alice arrived, and hastily taking off her coat, proceeded into the dining room to check the table and the cutlery. Then she made for the oven. 'What's cooking?' she said.

'Beef Wellington,' Ruth said.

'Alice raised her eyebrows. 'Special occasion?' she said.

'Sort of,' Ruth said. 'Will Jim see to the drinks?'

'Sure, Ma,' Jim said.

Fran and Alistair arrived, then Martin, whom Alice scrutinised closely.

'This is Alice, my daughter, Martin Amesbury.'

Alice's green eyes were quite frosty.

'He keeps that nice antiques shop in the village,' Ruth said.

And Alice's one dimple appeared. 'How do you do, Martin,' she said ...